CAPTURED AMONG THE STARS

BY C. M. LOCKHART

WRITTEN IN MELANIN

Established • 2019

THE LADY WIDOW

BOOK 2

For the Black girls who save themselves first.

OTHER BOOKS BY C. M. LOCKHART

The Lady Widow Series

Death Among the Stars

Wrath of the Gods Trilogy

We Are the Origin

We Are Dying Gods

Standalones and Anthologies

Keeping Promises

Magic in the Melanin: A Black Fantasy Anthology

Featured in

The Stygian Collection

FIYAH #32: Spacefaring Aunties

AUTHOR'S NOTE

Dear reader,

Thank you for picking up *The Lady Widow: Captured Among the Stars*. This book is the second installment of a novella series about a grieving widow who becomes the captain of her late husband's spaceship in order to avenge his murder. This is a linear series, so if you haven't already, it's recommended that you read *The Lady Widow: Death Among the Stars* first.

This series deals with themes of death, grief, substance abuse (smoking), and murder, so please be mindful of that as you continue this journey of unapologetic revenge. This book includes scenes of graphic violence, so please make the decision that is best for you and your mental health. An updated list of content warnings will be kept on my website at CMLockhart.com.

Enjoy.

PREVIOUSLY IN
THE LADY WIDOW

Kyra Johnson, a fresh widow, buried her husband, **Xavier,** on Earth. He was an alien who'd sailed through the stars as the captain of *The Reveler*. With his death weighing heavy on her heart and an invite from his first mate, **James**, Kyra takes to the stars with his crew as their new captain.

But she is, in no way, prepared for the responsibilities that come with being in charge. So, rather than lead the ship and its crew on their next journey, she hides herself away in the observatory of the ship — watching the stars and letting herself drown in grief. It is in that sunken place that she bonds with **Glupin**, the fire slime that blows relaxing smoke that smells of happier times, and **Pia**, the fifteen-year-old girl who serves as the ship's mechanic. Together, they bond over their shared misery and the heartache of their loss, but when Kyra gets a rude awakening, her world pivots.

Xavier's death was no accident, and when her mind clears, she sets her sights on the man who killed him.

With a new focus and determination driving her, Kyra abandons the observatory and the constant haze Glupin left her in. Instead, she begins training with **Sigurd** — a cyborg shipwright and close friend of Xavier's — to get revenge. Pia, still caught in the unrelenting clutches of grief, distances herself, but Kyra remains unfazed.

Armed with a new weapon, an upgraded translator, and brimming with a cold, calculating rage, Kyra flies to Zaigera and takes the life of **Howard Wright**. But he was just the first to fall on her road to revenge. Kyra plans to snuff out every life that played a part in taking her husband away from her, including **Epidemic**, the mastermind behind it all.

With fresh blood on her hands, Kyra is rebranded as *The Lady Widow*, and she sets a course for Shereve in the Minotosah Galaxy to collect the bounty on Howard Wright's head and the memories lingering in his brain…

13 DAYS A LADY

"I thought you'd given up smoking in the observatory?"

I opened my eyes and let them roam over Sigurd. His six-two frame filled the small doorway by the stairs as he studied me with crossed arms. Part of me wanted to explain myself — that I'd come up here to get a break from him and James and their hellish training. I was grateful to them both, but if James made me decipher one more map littered with foreign stars and alien text, I'd be cross-eyed for the rest of my life. I just needed a moment to catch up to myself, but that explanation wouldn't go over well with Sigurd, and a much larger part of me enjoyed pushing his metaphorical buttons. It was amusing to watch the dark blue hues of his cybernetic eyes and joints light up with frustration. So, I smiled and shrugged at him instead.

"Aw. You worried about me, Siggy?"

"Don't call me that."

"You love that name," I said, laughing as I struck a match and fed it to Glupin. When he didn't move to sit down, I rolled my eyes and gestured to the free seat across from me. "You can sit down, you know? This is only his second match, and I haven't fed him in over ten cycles. It's fine."

"Him?" Sigurd asked, lifting his brows as his lips twitched. "You can tell them apart now?"

"Yes?"

I frowned, unsure of what Sigurd meant. Glupin had always seemed like an it before — more an orange plushie rather than a living being — but the more time I spent with Glupin, the less he felt like a thing and more like a companion. It didn't feel right to keep objectifying him. Not when he clearly liked me and glubbed so sweetly whenever I held onto him and squished his little form in my hands. He was adorable and loyal, and I loved him.

"I mean, Glupin is clearly a boy."

"Sure he is," Sigurd chuckled. "If you say so."

"Can you tell them apart?" I asked, getting irritated by Sigurd's smug attitude.

"Slimes don't take on a gender until they bond with a host," he stated, moving to sit on the bench next to me and stretching out his long legs in front of him. "And then they take on whatever gender their host sees them as. So, if you say Glupin is a boy," he said, squishing his fingers gently into Glupin's round form as he glubbed out a fresh stream of smoke, "he's a boy. You would know better than anyone else."

"That's kinda cool," I said, grinning at Glupin as I picked him up. "I didn't know that about you."

He glubbed again, and the smoke in the room smelled of warm

apple cider, cinnamon, freshly baked bread, and cream cheese icing. I inhaled a deep breath and smiled at the memory of warm cinnamon rolls that Glupin gave me. I sank into it for a moment, closing my eyes and drifting back to softer days of baking in my kitchen, wearing oversized sweaters, and sipping spiked cider with Xavier. Moments like that were what I missed most about him sometimes. And though I was grateful to Glupin for breathing life back into the memories for me, sometimes, my throat got thick thinking of what would never be again.

It was better some days, but others I'd be left a blubbering mess and, for once, I was glad that I wasn't alone — that Sigurd was with me. He wasn't my favorite person on the ship, but we understood each other. Quiet moments with him were always comfortable rather than awkward.

He never felt the need to fill the silence with pointless chatter.

So, I took a moment to let myself breathe through the memory. To remember Xavier and our life together. To be grateful for every moment we had and to be heartbroken over the memories we'd never be able to create. It was a process, and Sigurd sat in silence next to me as I closed my eyes and worked through the waves of emotions crashing into me.

Maybe he had his own thoughts about missing Xavier — Captain Zay, as he and the rest of the crew had known him — but we never spoke about that. And maybe that's why I appreciated the silence with Sigurd. He understood some things weren't meant to be shared with everyone. That there were some things we held on to, just for ourselves.

He never pushed me to share my memories of Xavier, and I never pried for his.

We worked best like that.

Once Glupin's smoke dissipated, I returned my attention to Sigurd. He was bent over, with an elbow on his knee as he watched the stars on the display panels in front of us. They were like giant windows scattered across the ship, and the observatory had the biggest one — a wall of panels that showed us the galaxy of pink and purple planets we drifted through. I'd gotten used to the constant dark of space punctuated by the blinding light of passing stars, but I still struggled not to associate the changes with day and night. I had to remember that the ship had its own concept of time and daily routines. It helped that the cycles on *The Reveler* were about as long as one day on Earth, but there were still more than sixty cycles left before we would reach Shereve in the Minotosah Galaxy.

Sixty cycles left before we would reach the one person who could steal back all the secrets the dead took with them.

It had been James' idea to take Howard Wright's severed head to Shereve and find out all that he knew. He'd taken the first steps down this bloody path of revenge with me and was doing his best to make sure I was prepared for it. So, I tried not to complain about my training with him. I knew his intention was to equip me with the skills I needed to keep myself alive, so I'd done my best to identify as many of the planets we sailed through as I could. I was getting better, but I still had a long way to go before I had a casual knowledge of them the way he did.

And sitting here, taking an extended break wasn't going to get me any closer to his level.

It was time for me to go back — I knew that — but talking with the crew was important too, and Sigurd would never come looking for me without a reason, so I stretched my arms above me as I looked at him.

"Why'd you come up here?" I asked. "I doubt all you wanted was my company."

"I was hoping to find Pia up here," he admitted. "But clearly she's not and isn't coming."

"She avoiding you now too?"

"Seems like it," he said, shrugging.

"I'm worried about her," I said, returning my attention to the stars. "Distancing yourself from people you care about isn't normal behavior."

"She'll be fine."

"You sure about that?" I asked, lifting a brow at him. "You sound a little too confident for someone who doesn't even know where she is."

"She's somewhere on the ship," he said, dismissing my words with a shrug. When I scoffed, Sigurd turned his head to frown at me. "What?"

"You're talking about her as if her feelings don't matter."

"Of course her feelings matter. But she's a child," he said, lifting his brows as if I needed to be reminded of how young Pia was. "And right now she's acting like one. But she'll bounce back soon enough. She's just unmoored without her captain."

I let out a noncommittal hum as I shrugged, swallowing the disappointment that wanted to clog my throat at the casual reminder that I wasn't seen as the captain of the ship — I only held the title for it. "I don't know if death is something you just bounce back from, Siggy."

"It is something that grows with you," he said, his voice gentle. "Your world has to expand beyond the grief until it's only a part of who you are and not the entirety of your being. And lucky for you," he said, glancing at me, "and for Pia," he added, "there's an entire universe lying in wait for you."

"That's a positive way to look at it."

"It's the only way to look at it," he corrected. "And if Pia needs our help remembering that her world is bigger than what she's feeling right now, we'll be there for her. But until she's ready, all we can do is give her some space. We can't force her to heal on our schedules."

"That's true," I conceded, thinking of the months I'd been little more than a comatose zombie — high off Glupin's smoke and locked in an emotional prison of my own making. I'd barely spoken to anyone. So, I couldn't really blame Pia if she didn't want to talk to anyone. It was frustrating being on the outside of it, but I respected it as part of the process and sighed as I nodded my head. "I'll be patient."

"Great," Sigurd said, reaching out to squeeze my shoulder in an awkward display of concern before dropping his hand. "If that's settled, then I'm going back to wo—"

The Reveler tilted in a way that was unnatural. Sigurd slid across the bench, his body crashing into mine as we slammed into the wall behind me. His forehead bumped into mine, and we both hissed in pain as he braced himself, pressing his palms into either side of the wall behind me.

Heat rolled off his brown skin as his blue eyes darted upward. Orange lights were flashing, and the same serene voice that announced our takeoffs and descents informed us that we were now under enemy fire. Sigurd sucked his teeth, and his blue eyes pinned me to the spot as he lifted his voice over the alarm.

"Where's your bracelet?"

I glanced down at my wrist and felt my heart drop. We were expected to be onboard for a few months before docking again, so I'd left Mandy — the name I'd affectionately given to my stythe — back in my room. Our next training session was hours away, and I didn't think I needed to carry a weapon around with me on board, so all I could do was shake my head at Sigurd.

He sucked his teeth again and sighed as the gravity control of the ship recalibrated. He pushed away from me, grabbed Glupin, and shoved him into my hands.

"Don't let go of him and follow me."

He took off jogging down the stairs, and I huffed as I pushed to my feet and stumbled across the observatory after him, the last traces of Glupin's smoke making my first few steps unsteady. But I knew he'd never slow down for me, so I sprinted down the stairs in an effort to keep up with him.

"Where are we going?"

"Control room," Sigurd shouted back, giving me a straight answer for the first time in his life. "Without Captain Zay, James can't fight."

The other questions I might have had stuck in my chest. The stories Xavier had regaled me with came flooding back, and I realized they may not have been as exaggerated as I once thought. My heart jumped into my throat at that realization, and I tightened my grip on Glupin as I sped up, doing my best to keep pace with Sigurd.

"I'm behind you!"

Sigurd led us through the flurry of bodies to the control room. The crew was picking up their weapons and gathering in the atrium to wait for orders, but the residents were locking their doors and shutting themselves inside their homes as giant metal doors came down in the hallways, sealing off each sector.

"What's happening?" I asked, my eyes growing wide as Sigurd grabbed my hand and yanked me under the door sliding into place between Sectors 2 and 3.

"Lockdown," he answered, keeping a firm grip on my hand as he pushed our way through the crowds rushing in every direction. "It keeps the residents safe so the crew can fight."

It was a simple explanation, and I was reminded of an early lesson with James, when he explained the roles of everyone on the ship. The crew was necessary to keep the ship running, but the residents were what kept the finances of *The Reveler* strong. We transported people and cargo through space, and we needed the economy in Sectors 4 through 8 to keep credits flowing through the ship. A portion of every market sale went toward the ship as a sort of tax, and that kept us from being overly reliant on any one company for work. It allowed us the freedom to accept or decline whatever work requests we wanted.

If the residents died, *The Reveler* would cease to exist.

Or, at the very least, be unable to travel through space with as much ease as we do. But financial logistics aside, none of us wanted to see anyone on the ship get hurt. So, the lockdown procedures were in place to keep everyone safe. If anyone did breach the ship, they'd be met in Sector 10 and funneled to either Sector 9 or Sector 1 — away from any stragglers who may not have gotten back home before their Sector was sealed off. In those cases, most of them sought shelter in Sector 3 until the fighting was over.

It was a system that had been fine-tuned over the centuries, but it still felt like a madhouse with everyone rushing around, and my heart nearly choked me to death before we even reached the control center. But when the doors hissed open, it was like stepping out of a burning circus into a tranquil office.

The triplets, Karmen, Keelah, and Kavira — the navigators who were of no blood relation — tapped away at their consoles. James stood in the center of the crescent, looking more like the captain than the first mate. He kept his hands in his pockets as he surveyed the chaos outside from a dozen different screens shifting before him. When Sigurd and I stepped inside, he grinned and stepped over to us, pulling Sigurd into one of those man hugs, the kind that's a mix between a dap and a pat on the back. It was something he had to have picked up on Earth, and it was such an unexpected normalcy that I almost felt homesick for a moment. It helped to calm my racing heart, and I followed them inside as James tapped on the console screen in the center — the one meant for the captain — and enlarged our view of a giant ship blocking our path forward.

It looked straight out of a sci-fi movie, with all types of thrusters and lasers, and I worked to pull in deep breaths to steady my racing heart. The ship was nothing if not intimidating, and the thought of being in a fight with them fed my anxiety in ways I didn't appreciate. But I seemed to be the only one fighting off waves of panic. Everyone else seemed unbothered, as if this were as routine as docking the ship at a nearby planet for lunch.

"I'm glad you're here," James said, letting his dark gaze bounce between Sigurd and me. "Although I wasn't expecting to see you two together."

When it became clear Sigurd wasn't going to offer up an explanation, James turned his gaze to me, and I shrugged.

"Do I need a reason to talk to someone?"

"No," James said, lifting his brows and making the word almost sound like a question. "I'm just surprised. Either way, it's convenient for me."

"What do you need?" Sigurd asked.

"For the captain to take the helm," James said, turning to face me.

"You mean me," I said, biting my lip. I'd gotten used to the title over the past week. Ever since I'd killed Howard Wright, James had been consistent in referring to me by my title in front of other people, but it still felt too big for me. The crew knew me as the Lady of the ship, and I preferred that distinction over the title of captain, but this was no time to be delicate about what people called me. So, I took a steadying breath and turned to meet James' gaze.

"What do you need me to do?"

"Watch everything," James said, pointing to the monitors, "and give the orders."

"What orders?"

"Whatever feels right," he said, sliding his hands back into his pockets. "I've gone over the protocols with you, and we've practiced the simulations. The only thing left is the real thing. But if you don't feel comfortable with that…"

"I'll be fine," I assured him. "This is my job. And," I said, glancing around to the three women surrounding us, "it's not like I'll be here alone."

And that much was true.

James had always believed in my ability to lead the crew — had never doubted Xavier's decision to leave me in charge of the home they'd built among the stars. But everyone hadn't shared his sentiments, and it hadn't helped that I'd been drowning in my grief when I arrived. The triplets, especially, had been harsh doubters of my future aboard *The Reveler* and hadn't been shy about voicing their distrust of me during my training sessions with James.

Respect was a thing earned on this ship, and they'd had none to spare for me. I'd used up all the grace they'd been willing to offer me as Xavier's widow when we'd landed in the Pursinian Galaxy and I'd refused to get off the ship, defying James' warning about Glupin and nearly killing myself in the process.

It wasn't until I returned to the control center, clear-headed and with an apology, that any of them were willing to spare me a second glance. In the days that passed, I'd gotten to know Karmen, Keelah, and Kavira on an individual basis and understood that they were more than just navigators — they were the eyes, ears, and voice of the crew.

From the control center, they could see every corner of the ship that wasn't a private residence. They saw the people, bore witness to their lives, listened to their woes, and advocated on their behalf when necessary. They were the intermediaries of the ship and had been fielding more than a few disgruntled and anxious complaints about the new leadership. But the rules of the ship were clear — I was the captain until I died or disbanded the crew, just as James had told me on the very first day I arrived.

So, I was determined to be better than I was.

I'd come to the control center every day. I'd studied under James, asked questions, and learned about every aspect of the ship I could. I read the maps, memorized the planets, learned about the ship, its history, and everywhere it had been. Not just so that Xavier's memory wouldn't be tainted by my failure, but because I wanted to be the leader they deserved.

If I was going to ask them to turn away from a peaceful existence of transportation and deliveries to tread one of blood and carnage, the least I could do was be reliable, understand the job, and show up for work.

So, I nudged James with a sharp elbow and a tiny smirk when he lifted his brows at me in a silent question: *Are you sure?*

"I'll be fine," I repeated, placing Glupin on the edge of the center console. "Go do what you have to do. I'll be here when you get back."

"Understood," James said, stepping back from the center of the crescent and smirking at me. "Captain at the helm!"

"Captain at the helm!" the triplets repeated in unison.

With those words, Sigurd and James nodded at me, warned me to be careful, and rushed out of the room. In their absence, I was reminded that I now had direct command of the ship. That made my heart pound twice as hard in my chest, but I'd known this day would come, eventually. It was nothing like my training sessions when I had the comfort of James's presence standing next to me, but instead of falling into a panic, I pulled out the chair in the center of the console — the one meant for the captain — and sank into it.

It was huge and navy blue and still smelled faintly of Xavier.

I took a deep breath and held it in. I was both grateful that this small piece of the ship still carried the memory of him, and angry with myself for always denying his invitations for adventure. But the past would forever remain unchanged, and this wasn't the moment to lose myself to thoughts of what could have been. So, I released the breath I'd been holding and rolled back my shoulders, getting comfortable in Xavier's chair.

"I'll be relying on you three to get me through this," I said, stretching out my fingers and letting them hover over the glowing buttons as James had taught me to do. "I'll do my best not to slow you down."

"Understood. We're ready when you are, *Captain.*"

It was Karmen who spoke the words, but both Kavira and Keelah nodded in unison. It was a small acknowledgement, but it was a huge step forward for all of us, and I couldn't stop the tiny smile that pulled at the corner of my lips.

"Alright," I said, returning their nods before focusing my attention on the screens the triplets pulled up in front of me. "Then let's do it. Talk me through this."

The next twenty minutes felt like twenty years.

The triplets talked me through each scene that popped up before me — showing me first the main corridors and sectors that were locked down. We confirmed that all the travelers were safe in secured areas before moving on to Sector 10.

I'd always known the sector was huge. It served as an outer shell for the ship, and it's where the engineers, mechanics, and shipwrights that Chise, Pia, and Sigurd oversaw did most of their work. Now, though, it was a battlefield.

The hangar bay, where the smaller ships with lasers were stored, had been cleared out — all of them zipping and zooming through space between our ship and *The Croceria* as they fired at the enemy. We were outnumbered, though, and the empty bay was the perfect location for the enemy to breach *The Reveler*.

They spilled out of their ships and onto ours, sending our warning signals from an intense orange to an urgent red. A siren blared, and my eyes darted up to the new screen that popped up in front of me. The attack squad that had been left in reserve on the ship ran to intercept the intruders, and I sucked down a steadying breath.

The purpose behind this attack was unclear, and unlike the movies I'd seen growing up, there was no tension strung out between us as we hailed the other ship and demanded answers. There was only action, and theirs spoke louder than any words.

They weren't here to make friends.

Regardless of what their motives were, our goals were clear: keep them locked down at the hangar bay and stop them from infiltrating deeper into the ship at all costs.

James and Sigurd led the charge, firing lasers and ripping through our enemies. There was no hesitation in their movements, only pure determination, and my breath caught in my throat at the sight. I'd never seen an actual battle where people were being vaporized in real time by icy-blue lasers, and my eyes were saucers glued to the displays.

James and Sigurd shouted orders to the crew on the front lines, which left me in charge of the defensive squad protecting the ship's inner sectors — because despite the skill that James, Sigurd, and everyone else displayed by pushing back the enemy, a handful of them managed to get past them and infiltrate the ship.

Minutes stretched out like eons as warriors with gray scales forced their way deeper into *The Reveler*, breaking through to Sector 9 and bearing down on the first line of defenders with sharpened claws. The enemy looked like overgrown crocodiles in navy blue tactical gear. They were powerful, but they didn't know the ship and that worked to our benefit.

"Tell Unit C to fall back," I said, infusing my voice with more confidence than I'd ever felt in my life. "There's an escape hatch down corridor 3," I said, glancing at the ship's map and silently thanking Sigurd and Chise for explaining to me how to read the pink holodisplays. "Have them meet with Unit A there. We can seal off the corridor once they arrive, open the hatch, and yeet both sets of crocs into space."

"What did you call them?" Kavira asked, her brown eyes dancing over to me for a moment. "And what is a 'yeet'?"

"They're Earth terms," I said, brushing off her question. "Show me Unit D on the south side of Sector 10," I said. "With Units A and C freed up, we might be able to divide and conquer the crocs that are left. Take them three on one."

"You heard her," Karmen said, speaking into the display. "Divide and conquer! And keep your heads on your shoulders at all costs!"

The next few minutes carried on like that, with me giving orders in an effort to keep the crew alive and the triplets conveying them. The ship was massive though, and I felt like I was barking orders nonstop. Most of them made sense. Some of them — like cornering the crocs in the sub-kitchens of Sector 9 and throwing the equivalent of hot grits at them — were a bit unorthodox. But soon the ship was still, the alarms and lights gone as we confirmed *The Reveler* was free of any surviving crocs.

I was making a final cycle through the observation displays when a girl with a messy bun, baggy overalls, and panicked violet eyes caught my attention as she sprinted down a corridor from the mech room toward the hangar bay. A grisly croc that was twice the size of the others lumbered down the hallway after Pia, and I slammed my hands into the console as I jumped to my feet.

"Where is she?"

Everyone in the room understood my question and began swiping across their screens to give me an answer. Keelah was the first to respond.

"The west side of Sector 10."

"What is she doing all the way over there?" I asked, shaking my head. "The hangar bay is to the north. How'd it get this far in?"

"Escape hatch," Kavira said, pulling up a screen showing a hastily patched hole on the far side of the ship. "Looks like it pried it open with its claws and climbed up while everyone else was focused on the hangar bay and other sectors. I don't know why the alarms didn't sound…"

"Can we get her out?" I asked. "Seal the croc down there alone until someone can reach them?"

"Unlikely," Keelah said, shaking her head. "It would take too long to lock down Sector 10."

"Are you telling me there's no way to get her out?" I asked, scouring the holodisplay map for an exit. "There's a door not too far from where she is that leads to Sector 5."

"With all due respect, Captain," Karmen said, choosing her words with care, "that would endanger all the residents on board. It would be unwise to lead it further inside the ship."

"So, you just want to abandon her?"

"She is one crew member weighed against hundreds of non-combatants, Lady Kyra," Keelah said, her tone icy as she interjected. "This isn't what we desire, but this is the nature of being the captain of this ship," she said. "Power and privilege come with responsibility and hard decisions. This is one of them."

I bit my lip in frustration and stood in silence, thinking of all the reasons why Keelah was right. Her logic was sound. In the grand scheme of the ship, even with all her brilliance, Pia was still just one girl. And in their eyes, I'm sure she could be replaced.

But Pia was the one who had kept me company during the worst days of my life. Who had climbed the stairs of the observatory and listened to my stories of Xavier when everyone else had been content to let me rot in my misery. She was the one who'd designed and crafted a weapon meant especially for me — the one who'd noticed how much I hated my translator and modified it into something I could comfortably wear — the one who'd given me directions when I was running from the enforcement squad on Zaigera, and she was the one who needed me the most right now.

There would always be someone looking out for the best interests of the ship.

Right now, my job was to look out for her. Because who would if I didn't?

"I understand what you're saying," I said, nodding at Keelah.

"Great," she said, sighing. "Then we can —"

"But I don't agree with it," I continued. "I'm not going to stand here and pretend I don't see her when she needs help." I shook my head. "I know you three will do what's best for the ship. Continue to do that until James returns."

"And what are you going to do?" Kavira asked. "You're not a fighter, Lady Kyra."

"No, but I'm not going to just abandon her either," I said, reaching out for Glupin.

He'd been glubbing quietly on the console next to me, and with the slightest invitation, he launched into the air and crawled over my shoulder to cling to my back. He was squishy and warm, and his presence startled me a bit — I didn't know slimes could jump like that — but I refused to flinch, yelp, or show any sign of weakness in front of the triplets. So, I ignored him and strode toward the exit.

"Is the gravity control still intact?"

"Yes," Karmen said. "Why?"

"I'm going to Sector 10," I stated. "And from here, it's faster if I just jump."

I didn't stay to hear any more words of dissent from the triplets. All I had in mind were three things.

Grab my bracelet.

Find Pia.

Kill the croc.

The tasks sounded far simpler in my head than I imagined they would actually be, but I knew that if I stopped to consider what kind of situation I was walking myself into, I'd doubt myself. I'd doubt my decision to save Pia and my ability to do it. And I didn't want that. Because even if I couldn't save her, it wouldn't be because I didn't try.

It wouldn't be because I abandoned her like the triplets seemed to be okay doing.

So, once I'd bounded out of the control room, I stepped over to the nearest railing and hoisted myself up on top of it. I'd seen others use the gravity control of the ship like a broken elevator, but jumping didn't feel any smarter when I was staring over the edge.

But the control center was in Sector 3, near the top of the ship. My room was in Sector 9 and Pia was in Sector 10. If I wanted to get to her with half the ship on lockdown, the fastest way would be to jump.

There was no time for my fear of heights to hold me back.

"You jump, I jump, Jack."

I spoke the words to no one in particular but saying them aloud was enough to give me the burst of courage I needed to fling myself over the side.

And, at first, it was terrifying. The wind rushed through my hair and through my ears, and snatched all my thoughts from me. I wanted to scream.

But instead of terror, laughter bubbled up from me.

And my eyes widened at the sound. Glupin jiggled on my back in what I could only assume was delight, and I relinquished my hold on all the things I'd been desperately clinging to for dear life.

My sanity.

My expectations.

The memories of my husband.

I was freer than I'd ever been. And something about laughing while free-falling through a spaceship in the midst of an epic space battle brought a clarity to my mind I'd never felt before.

This is what Xavier had wanted to give me.

Just being in the stars wasn't enough.

I had to revel among them.

I finally understood what that meant.

But no sooner than I'd figured that out, was I slowing down, and my feet were brushing against the floor. I was on the bottom floor of *The Reveler*, and there was no time to waste.

The lockdown had put most of the lights on the ship at half capacity to conserve energy and funnel every drop of power that was needed to the ship's defensive shields. Every step I took seemed to echo down the hall, and a chill raced up my spine as I dashed into my room, scooping my bracelet off my desk and slapping it on my wrist.

"Now, to find Pia."

I'd barely taken two steps back into the hallway when the metal divider separating Sectors 9 and 10 screeched as a gaping hole was ripped into it. Before I could even think to scream, a scaly hand wrapped around my throat. It lifted me off my feet and slammed me into the wall behind me, knocking all the wind and good sense out of me. I felt Glupin glub and squish beneath me before he spread out, wrapping himself around my chest like a vest. I heaved and clutched at the hard, scaly hand, blinking a thousand times to try and clear my vision as the massive crocodile came into view.

It stood on two legs like a man, but it was all beast. It wore a navy-blue tactical suit like the others, but its shiny scales were pitch black and frigid against my skin. I shivered as I squirmed beneath its grasp, trying to free myself.

"Who…"

"I am Zentrith," it hissed at me. "And you've upset the boss. So, you're coming with me."

My eyes glanced around, desperate to find anyone I could call out to for help, but all I saw was Pia's slumped-over body on the ground, being dragged behind the massive crocodile by its tail. Her neck sported the same bruises I would no doubt have soon, and I tried to reach for my bracelet — for a way to fight back. But it was a pointless endeavor. Before I could, Zentrith was pulling me from the wall and hissing again.

"Enough of that. Sleep."

With that, he tightened his grip on my neck and slammed me against the wall twice. The first time, I loosened my grip on him, and my thoughts darted to Pia — how I managed to not only fail at saving her, but get myself captured, too. I almost wanted to laugh at myself. I'd tried to be a hero like Xavier, and now I was either going to die or become someone's hostage.

James was going to be furious.

Zentrith slammed me into the wall again and finally — mercifully — everything went black.

A LADY TAKEN

My mind divorced my body three times.

The first time was nothing but quiet bliss. I saw nothing — heard nothing — felt nothing. I was an untethered soul in space, and it was a quiet kind of wonder. I could have stayed that way forever, and not a single word of complaint would have ever passed through my lips.

But nothing lasts forever.

For the briefest moments, my eyes fluttered open. Just long enough for the world to spin and my head to pound and my stomach to lurch as Zentrith tossed me into his space shuttle. I had enough sense not to scream, but the moment my body crashed against the ground — my head bouncing against the cold steel of the ship — my mind and body separated once more.

This time, I was a ghost — haunting myself.

I curled up next to my physical body and tried to pay attention to where he was taking us, but the battle between *The Reveler* and *The Croceria* was intense. Explosions rang out every five seconds, jostling the shuttle. We waded through ship wreckage and body parts from both sides, and though I couldn't tell who was winning this fight, I felt a little reassured whenever I saw the navy blue tactical suits of the crocs rather than the more casual clothes of the crew. But as we approached *The Croceria*, the Crocs pulled back, and what little hope I'd had that we'd be rescued during this battle burst in my chest and settled into dread at the pit of my stomach.

The Reveler was a civilian transport ship. They wouldn't pursue the Crocs. And even if they did, it wouldn't be until after they realized Pia and I were gone.

If they noticed at all.

Pia's absence would definitely be noticed. Sigurd and Chise would look for her immediately. But me? The crew might realize I was missing, but I'd be surprised if anyone other than James actually cared.

It was a depressing thought, but it was my own fault if no one on the ship missed me — I hadn't been the greatest captain. I'd only just begun learning the job, and my first decision was to take *The Reveler* to a planet outside of the KUAF and cut a man's head off. He'd deserved it, and no one had complained, but it wouldn't be winning me any Captain of the Year awards. And realizing that I likely wouldn't be missed clawed at tender places in my heart, ripping open fresh scars that had yet to heal.

Before I could get lost in a spiral of misery though, the shuttle jolted — tossing everyone around as it barrel-rolled off course. Zentrith growled as he clutched at the controls and tried to right the shuttle, but explosions were sounding off all around us again — closer this time — and we were being tossed around like waves on the sea. Pia and I slid around the back of the shuttle, helpless. I tried to will my body to wake up, to see the chaos around us and make the most of it to free us, but I was nothing more than dead weight slamming into the sides of the shuttle with every attack.

Static crackled over whatever communication device Zentrith had before a sharp voice cut through it.

"Where do you think you're going, Zentrith?"

Was that Sigurd?

"Get out of my way, dust-grubber," Zentrith hissed before firing off a string of missiles at the ship in front of us. It evaded the attack and returned fire on us with a pulsing stream of neon purple lasers, but Zentrith only laughed as he floored the shuttle. He jerked us through space, doing his best to avoid the lasers that attempted to cut through the creaking metal of the shuttle while still bringing us ever closer to the hangar bay of *The Croceria.*

For a moment, I was grateful that he was a decent pilot because Sigurd was a great shot. If even one of those lasers hit us, we'd all be sucked into the wide expanse of space, and none of us wanted that. But it wasn't lost on me that I was relying on my enemy to keep me safe from the only person who might attempt to rescue me.

The irony of it all was sickening.

For all of Zentrith's skills though, he wasn't a match for Sigurd. Not really. One of his laser shots nicked the shuttle's thrusters on the left and it exploded. Zentrith screamed — or maybe it was a growl of pure frustration — as we went spinning out of control. He tried to right us, but the shuttle was off balance and the momentum was too much for one thruster to combat alone.

Sigurd was already lining up another shot, but before he could fire it, Zentrith slammed a meaty claw onto his console and shouted at the top of his lungs.

"Is this how you want your captain to die, dust-grubber?" he asked, a sick grin spreading across his face as Sigurd hesitated. "Blasted into space? If you wanted her dead, you should've handled it yourself already."

"What are you talking about?"

"No clue about what's happening in your own house, do you?" he chuckled.

"What are you —"

Before Sigurd could repeat his question, we were both caught in a pale-yellow light that stopped the shuttle in an instant. Zentrith was locked into his seat, but Pia and I were thrown once more into the side of the shuttle. The last thing I saw was a ring of *Croceria* ships encircling Sigurd's. When my head slammed into the wall, everything went black once more.

"How long are you planning to sleep, Ky?"

The words were soft and husky and almost playful as a warm hand slid over my skin. It was comforting and I sighed as I wiggled my body closer, pressing my back into the hard lines of the man behind me like I'd done countless times before.

"Forever," I muttered back, fighting back a grin as soft kisses landed on the back of my neck and shoulder. His long fingers traced circles up and down my thigh as he chuckled.

"A shame," he whispered, sliding his hand up, over my hip and stomach. "I'd hoped we could spend some time together before I left today."

His hand cupped the soft curve it was searching for, and a mix between a giggle and a moan slipped out as he massaged it and continued to pepper my skin with kisses. I pried my eyes open and turned to face him, smiling up into his dark eyes as he captured my lips in a greedy kiss. He tugged me closer, and I melted into him before placing my hands on his chest and tugging away from him, just enough to catch my breath.

"I thought you weren't leaving until Wednesday?"

"That was the plan," he admitted, offering me a tiny smirk, "but someone said she wanted to go shopping in Concord Mills this weekend."

"You know I can take Jasmine with me," I said. "You don't have to change your plans for me."

"I can and I will," he said, kissing me again. "What is the point of having a beautiful wife if I can't spoil her with all the things she wants?"

I slid my hand down his body between us until my fingers wrapped around the hard length of him. He sucked in a slow breath as he bit his lip and held my gaze. It was my turn to smirk as I slid my hand over him and leaned closer.

"You know," I whispered, pecking his lips, "some would argue that there are other benefits to having a beautiful wife."

"And I plan to take full advantage of those as well," he whispered back, before gripping the back of my neck and pulling me in for another kiss.

Xavier always knew exactly how to make me lose my grip on reality, and this morning was no different. We stayed in bed until the golden streams of light that always fought their way through our curtains in the morning became nothing more than a pale bar of white afternoon light on the floor.

We were still wrapped around each other and cozied up beneath the covers when I finally managed to pull my eyelids apart again. He was snoring lightly next to me. Never too loud, but just enough that I always knew he was there. I smiled at his sleeping face and tried to burn every tiny detail of his face into my brain, running my fingers over his thick eyebrows and wide nose and full lips before placing a hand on his bald head and placing a kiss on his cheek.

"You're going to be late if you don't get up soon," I whispered.

He groaned and pulled me closer. "The captain is never late."

"I'm sure James would beg to differ."

"Good thing James isn't the captain then," he chuckled, burying his face in my shoulder.

"Zay…"

"Five more minutes," he hummed. "Then I'll get up."

"Fine," I said, giving in and settling back into the covers. "But don't blame me if he yells at you."

"Oh, I definitely will," he said, grinning. "I'll tell him my wife is a temptress and seductress and I had absolutely no chance of escaping her lustful clutches."

I barked out a laugh. "Me? I believe it was *you* who woke *me* up, sir."

"And yet I didn't hear a word of complaint from you," he murmured, kissing the base of my throat. "How odd."

"Oh, I was definitely a willing participant, don't get me wrong," I said, giggling. "But let you tell it and your crew will have all kinds of wrong impressions about me."

"If you came with me, they'd meet you and form their own impressions." He lifted his head and gave me a heart-stopping grin. "Come with me this time. It'll only be for a few days," he said. "Just to the edge of your solar system and back."

"I can't," I whispered, guilt blooming in my chest at the way the corners of his lips fell. "I already took today and tomorrow off so we could spend some time together before you left, but I thought you weren't leaving until Wednesday. I can't miss that many days at work without some kind of explanation."

He sighed and nodded, dropping the topic. He'd been asking me for years to go on a trip with him, but there never seemed to be a good time. Between work, caring for my aging parents, and supporting Jasmine with her son, there was never a good time to disappear for weeks or months at a time. But as Xavier pushed off the bed, I promised myself that I'd say yes to him one day. I'd quit teaching last year and become a financial advisor so that I'd have more sanity and a flexible schedule — nights that didn't require making lesson plans, weekends without grading papers, and summers that didn't require teaching summer school or preparing for the fall. I wouldn't live my entire life without ever seeing the stars from his point of view.

"You meeting with that same woman from before?" he asked, grabbing a towel and washcloth from the linen closet. "The one you helped with her taxes?"

"Yeah. She wants to start setting up for her retirement soon."

"Isn't she too young for that?"

"She's in her forties," I pointed out. "Most people start planning much earlier than that if they can afford to. No one wants to have to work until they're seventy."

"And that's considered old, right?"

"Most people don't make it past eighty-five, here."

"Hm." He paused by the door before offering me a weak smile. "Time disappears too quickly, here. I don't like it."

Before I could say anything else, he stepped inside the bathroom, and I snuggled back beneath the sheets, lazing in the warmth. I don't know how long I laid there, but it wasn't until I was being lightly shaken that I realized I'd fallen back asleep.

"I'm heading out, Ky," Xavier whispered. "I'll be back by Friday."

"Mm," I hummed, reaching out for him. He brought his face closer and placed a kiss on my forehead.

"Go back to sleep, babe," he whispered. "I love you."

"Love you," I whispered back. "Be safe."

"I always am."

Part of me wanted to push myself from the bed and chase after him. To cling to him a bit longer and tell him to wait for me. Tell him that I'd get dressed and go with him right now. That I would follow him anywhere. That I loved him more than anything in the universe and that I was sorry for always saying no. That I would give him whatever he wanted if he just stayed a bit longer. But my body was lead, and sleep was a crooning siren, desperate and impatient to drag me under her merciless waves.

I fought against the temptation, but it was pointless. No matter how hard I shoved it away from me — how hard my soul begged and pleaded with the universe not to drag me back to a darker, danker reality — my world fell back into darkness. I couldn't win.

Life was unforgiving that way.

4 HOURS

A CAPTIVE

When I woke up this time, it was to a blurry world and the worst headache of my life.

My vision jumped behind my eyelids with every pulse, and I prayed for the briefest moment that this was all just a nightmare. That if I pinched myself hard enough, I'd wake up in my bed at home. I'd be back on Earth in the tiny house on Wind Decker Drive with the blue door, creaky floors, and cozy bed with fluffy pillows and warm sheets. I'd laze around with no concept of what life in space was like. I'd scroll my phone and half-watch a movie until Xavier came home — and he would come home because he'd still be alive.

I'd be his wife, not his widow.

But there was no mistaking my cold reality for anything else.

This wasn't a dream and I couldn't wake up from it.

Every part of me wanted to wail like a newborn child in the face of that fact, but there was no point. Tears wouldn't bring Xavier back. If they could, he'd already be here. And without him, "home" was nothing more than a memory — a concept of a place that couldn't exist for me anymore. Wind Decker Drive was just an empty house I'd left behind on Earth. There was nothing to miss about it and nothing to go back to.

Which meant I could only look forward.

"Lady Kyra!"

I recognized Pia instantly. Even with my sight shifting and blurred and her voice clogged with panic, there was no mistaking her for anyone else. She hovered over me, shoving her tiny, calloused hands into my shoulder in a desperate attempt to wake me. And maybe it was because I was disoriented and probably concussed, but she seemed smaller to me than usual, like she'd shrunk down to half her size since I'd last seen her.

It was a stark reminder that she was a child.

A talented child with an attitude bigger than some of the solar systems we sailed through, but still a child. Pia carried so much responsibility on her shoulders that it was easy to forget how young she was. But other times, like now, it was impossible to see her as anything other than the panicked fifteen-year-old girl she was — scared out of her mind and doing her best to make it seem as if she wasn't making everything up as she went along.

She wasn't old enough yet to realize that's all any of us were doing.

Part of me wanted to reach out to her and tell her that I was okay — that we would be okay — but before I could, cold droplets were falling from her violet eyes and tapping against my cheeks. It was like a bucket of water had been tossed over me, and all the clarity I'd been fighting to regain rammed itself into me like a metal rod up my spine, and I coughed as I bolted upright.

"I'm up," I mumbled, pushing away her calloused hands. "Stop shaking me."

"Thank the stars," Pia whispered, throwing herself into me. "You weren't moving and I —"

Her voice cracked as she sobbed, and I froze under her sudden display of affection.

Pia had never hugged me before.

In fact, no one on *The Reveler* really came near me. Aside from Sigurd, who tossed me around the training hall like a ragdoll during our sparring sessions, and James, who'd caught me during my weakest moment, most everyone else kept their distance from me. I couldn't remember the last time someone had hugged me with such desperation, and my muscles were stiff as I wrapped my arm around Pia to pat her on the back.

"I'm fine," I promised. "Just a little banged up."

"Well, isn't that just the sweetest thing south of Gormander Prime."

The words were syrupy — sweet and intoxicating and made of the thickest southern accent I'd ever heard. It tugged at old memories of being a child drinking cold water from a hose outside in Georgia's summer heat. The nostalgia was suffocating, but it couldn't distract me from the poison lacing those words, and I shoved Pia behind me as I turned to face the body on the other side of the room.

To say the woman sitting there was beautiful would be an understatement. Even in the pale light filtering through the slitted windows above us, she looked ethereal. She had tawny brown skin, a ginger afro, full pink lips, bright hazel eyes, and freckles everywhere. They were like constellations down her arms and across her face, and she looked very much like a stolen princess in her dingy white sundress, open-toed sandals, and golden jewelry. She had a tiny golden orb pierced through her ear that lit up with pale green rings that chased after themselves at the slightest sound whenever someone spoke. I guessed it to be the same kind of translator Pia and I had — at least, it served the same function, even if it wasn't the same design.

Seeing hers jolted the foggy parts of my brain to clarity, and I glanced at Pia.

"Have you been able to reach anyone?" I asked, whispering the question to her as I touched a finger to the translator in my ear. She'd upgraded ours before we landed on Zaigera. The control center on *The Reveler* should be able to communicate with us and track our location, but the small shake of her head demolished whatever flimsy wisps of hope I'd been grasping for.

"Something's jamming the signal," she whispered back. "We're on our own."

"Would the two of you like to share with the rest of the class what you're whispering about over there?"

My eyes cut back across the room. Our cellmate looked unbothered, but I recognized the edge of irritation that had snuck into her words, even if her face remained as tranquil as ever. I wasn't surprised, though. She gave me the impression of a woman who dealt in falsehoods and facades — a woman who knew just how far her looks would get her. That kind of woman was dangerous, and I narrowed my eyes in suspicion when she smiled at us.

"I'm sorry," she said, glancing between me and Pia, "it was rude of me to cut into your conversation like that. It's been more than twenty cycles since I've had a proper conversation with anyone, and I guess my little feelings were bruised at seeing myself on the outside of an inside conversation."

She let out a soft laugh that would've smoothed over the situation had my brain not stalled out over her casual confession.

"Twenty cycles?" I repeated, lifting my brows.

"Give or take," she said, nodding with a shrug. "I don't have an exact number, of course, but I've been locked in here long enough." She chuckled and sat back, resting her head against the steel wall behind her. "Far too long, if you ask me."

"And where is 'here', exactly?" Pia asked from behind me. "Where are we?"

"Oh, I have no idea, jeiya," the woman said. "I see just as many exits as you do. All I can tell you," she said, gesturing around, "is that we're being held somewhere on *The Croceria*."

"And you've been in here for weeks…"

I whispered the words more to myself than anyone else in the room as I trailed my eyes over the woman again. It didn't make any sense for her to have been in here that long. Zentrith hadn't seemed the least bit hospitable when he was choking me half to death and tossing me into his shuttle. And based on our conditions in this cell — no chairs, beds, windows, food, water, and barely any light — the crocs weren't thoughtful captors. There wasn't so much as a toilet or sink in sight, but based on her appearance, I'd have never guessed that. She looked clean and composed as she smiled at us, and everything in me was set on edge.

"You don't look like you've been here for that long," Pia said, speaking my own thoughts out loud. I wanted to glare at her and warn her to be quiet, but there was something to be said about the innocence of children. It was disarming, and the woman on the other side of the room seemed to jump at the chance to keep talking.

"Why, thank you, jeiya," she said, giving us another blinding grin before smoothing her hand over her dress. "I managed to sweet-talk Zoek into letting me use a wash capsule. It's not much, but it's better than sitting in my own stink all day."

"Who's Zoek?" I asked.

"I guess you'd call her the guard?" She shrugged. "She brings food and water down here twice a cycle. She talks to me sometimes."

"And you can measure the cycles here?" Pia asked, looking around at the dim light filtering in. It was a pale shade of purple and, as far as I could tell, it hadn't shifted in the slightest since I'd woken up. "How?"

"Trade secret," the woman said, putting her finger to her lips. "But I can tell you that you were asleep for about four hours, and we have less than one before Zoek comes back around."

My heart raced in my chest at the thought of seeing another croc up close, and I resisted the urge to lift a hand to my throat. I could already feel the bruises there whenever I shifted my head even the slightest amount. Part of me wanted to get revenge against Zentrith — deprive him of oxygen and toss him around a metal box until he was blacking out and seeing his dead lover in his dreams. But when Pia squeezed my arm, I was reminded that I had more pressing issues.

One being that *The Reveler* wasn't just idling out in space.

We'd been headed for Shereve in the Minotosah Galaxy, and without the captain, the hierarchy of the ship would morph from a benevolent dictatorship to a ruthless democracy. The crew would vote on whether to change course or not, and considering how the triplets had reacted to the idea of trying to save Pia when we were still aboard the ship, I could only imagine how that vote would go. The thought alone sent ice crawling up my spine, and I tried not to let the jaws of panic close shut around me.

James would fight to rescue us, but his vote alone wasn't enough to overturn a majority rule. Our best hope was that he could at least slow down *The Reveler* and give us enough time to find our way back to it.

But on the off chance he couldn't, we needed to get a move on. Because if my math was right and this woman was to be trusted — and I wasn't fully convinced that she could be — then we only had eight hours left before *The Reveler* sailed on to brighter stars and left us behind.

Pia squeezed my arm again, and I blinked as I met her gaze. Her brows were squished together with concern, and I let the anxiety creeping onto my face slide away.

She didn't need to know that I was two seconds away from freaking out.

I was her captain. If I lost it, she would too, and there was no time for that. So, I turned back to the woman across the room and offered a polite smile.

"I appreciate the information," I said, trying to keep my words even and inject them with the sincerity I felt. "Thanks for the heads up."

"Heads up?" she repeated, her perfect brows pulling together. "I'm not sure I know what that means."

"Thanks for making us aware," Pia explained, glancing up at me. "It's a local idiom."

"Oh! Well, of course! We're here together now, aren't we?"

"Yeah," I said, dragging out the word and trying to force my body to relax a bit. I didn't trust her as far as I could throw her, but she was right — we were here together, and if we were going to get off of this ship, at the very least, we didn't need to make an enemy of her before we had a chance to make her an ally. "What's your name?"

"I am Shyanne Olight," she said, sitting up straight and placing her fist over her heart. "First Commander of the *AFS Althea*. At your service."

"Kyra Johnson," I said, introducing myself. "Captain of *The Reveler*. And this is Pia."

Her eyes went wide.

"*The Reveler*, you said?"

"That's the one," I said, nodding.

"I'm sorry but…" she shook her head and blinked her hazel eyes a few times too fast. "I thought Captain Zay stood at the helm of *The Reveler*. Is it perhaps a different ship with the same name?"

"No," I said, sighing and letting my shoulders fall. "Xavier's dead. I'm his wife. And *The Reveler* is my ship now."

"He had *a wife?*"

Shyanne had been whispering some version of that to herself over and over again for the past twenty minutes. At least, that's how long it felt. I had no way to keep track of the time the way she did, but her obsession with Xavier having been married was an upgrade from the shock of her finding out about his death. Hearing her whisper, "Zay's *dead?*" a million times over had been torture — a death by a thousand cuts.

It was easier to ignore her now, and my focus was on the door Zoek was rumored to be coming through and gaining my bearings.

The cell wasn't big. A cube that was just tall enough for us to stand up in. If I lifted onto my toes, the top of my head would slam into the ceiling. It wasn't wide either — barely more than twelve feet in each direction. That wasn't enough space for me to use Mandy to fight our way out.

Definitely not enough space to overpower a croc.

My eyes glanced at the slitted windows at the top of the cell, but they weren't much use either. I'd be lucky to squeeze a hand through the thin slats, let alone fit one of us through it. I slid a hand into my afro and tugged at my roots in frustration as I paced in a tight circle — two steps to the left and back again. But that wasn't helping, so I just slumped back down to the ground and closed my eyes.

Getting out of here was not going to be easy.

I glanced over at Pia and felt my chest tighten. She had her knees pulled up to her chest, and it was obvious she'd been crying at some point. Her violet eyes were puffy, and the faded green ribbon that normally held back her messy curls was knotted in her hair and dangled by her shoulder. It left her dark brown curls flowing out from her head like tendrils of chaos. She sported angry purple bruises around her throat that matched my own, and I tried to encourage her as I bumped my shoulder into hers.

"Everything will be fine," I said, trying to believe my own lie. "We'll get out of this."

"You don't know that," she said, hiding her face in her knees with a heavy sigh. "You should've never come after me, Lady Kyra."

Her words made me freeze. They were heavy — too heavy. They were sad and dull and carried the exhaustion of two lifetimes. It made me want to reach out and hug her, but I didn't. Instead, I reached over and began working the knots out of her hair as best I could to free her ribbon.

"What are you talking about? Of course, I came after you," I said, shrugging. "I would never leave you to fend for yourself."

And those words were true. Even though I hadn't known her long, Pia was important to me. It was almost shocking to admit that to myself — to put the feelings into words — and I wanted to laugh at myself. Apparently, jumping from the third floor of *The Reveler* to fight a giant alien crocodile with no plan wasn't enough to prove I cared about her. It wasn't until we were sitting in a prison cell on an enemy ship that I dared to identify my most basic emotions. It was comical, honestly. But when I'd seen Pia running for her life, I hadn't thought twice about going after her — about putting myself between her and the monster chasing her.

Reflecting on the moment made all kinds of complicated emotions rise to the surface, and my stomach twisted in uncomfortable directions with embarrassment. I'd really thought I could save her — that I could protect her when I could barely protect myself. I couldn't help but cringe at how inflated my ego was, and I was glad she couldn't see my face as

I tried to tame her curls without a comb, brush, or water. I managed to corral them into a messy bun that somewhat resembled her normal style, but detangling that mass of hair would be a nightmare later. It was better than what it was before, though. Zentrith had done a number on both of us, and my chest burned with shame and rage that he'd been able to shut me down without any effort at all. I sucked in a deep breath as I sat back and tugged at my afro again, shoving the memories of those last moments aboard *The Reveler* aside.

I didn't regret chasing after Pia. She'd taken up space with me when my misery had needed company, and she'd shown up for me in ways no one else had. When James had been content to watch over me from afar — when Sigurd had been frustrated with how long it was taking me to process my grief — when the triplets made it clear they wanted James to be captain of the ship rather than me — it was Pia who acknowledged me with all my broken parts. Of all the crew members aboard *The Reveler*, Pia was one of the few who saw me as *Kyra* rather than *Captain Zay's wife*.

That meant something to me.

"Even if you feel like you've got no one else, you've got me," I said, my stomach flipping with how cheesy the words felt leaving my lips. But I didn't know any better way to communicate to her that she wasn't alone than to just say it. "I'm always going to be here for you. We're in this together."

"Don't say that," she whispered, sucking in a shaky breath. "Just… don't. I'm not that important, Lady Kyra."

"Don't you ever say that again," I said, working to keep my voice even. "That you're not important."

"I'm not!"

"You are," I said, holding her gaze. "You're part of the only family I have in space, Pia." I admitted, stating the obvious. "Without Xavier, you and James are all I have now. And Sigurd too, I guess," I added, coughing out a laugh to try and lighten the suddenly serious mood. "But only on the days he can muster up the energy to be nice to me."

She shook her head, her violet eyes brimming with fresh tears as she looked at me.

"You wouldn't say that if you knew the truth," she whispered, her voice hoarse.

"And what truth is that?"

"I can't be your family, Lady Kyra," she said, her words punctuated by a sob she tried and failed to contain.

"Why not?" I asked, placing a gentle hand on her shoulder. "Talk to me."

"You wouldn't need a new family in space if it weren't for me."

"I don't understand."

"It's me," she said, closing her eyes and flinching away from my hand until it fell from her shoulder. "I'm the reason Captain Zay is dead," she said, sobbing. "So… you… you can't…" she shook her head, tears streaming down her face that was scrunched up in the most apologetic look I'd ever seen. "You can't… be so nice to me. I…" she paused to sob again, and I just stared at her with wide eyes. "I can't… be the reason… our ship… loses you too," she wailed, swiping at her eyes and hiding her face in her knees again.

I sat there, rooted to the spot and unable to comprehend her words, though they played like a broken record in my mind. It was like time stopped as I stared at her. Every nerve in my body stood on end and the oxygen in the room disappeared.

I struggled to draw in a breath.

I knew I should say something, anything, but before I could even form coherent thoughts, Shyanne launched herself across the small space and pinned Pia to the ground. She ignored all of Pia's sobs and weak attempts to get away, her hazel eyes shifting into something feral as she snarled at Pia.

"What do you mean, you're the reason Zay is dead!?"

It took three very long breaths for my mind and body to coordinate with each other.

The first breath, I was filled with nothing but rage.

I couldn't help it.

As much as I'd grown to adore Pia, I loved Xavier — and Pia had just rammed a pillar of salt into wounds that were still bleeding and raw to the touch. I wanted answers from her.

The second breath, I went numb.

Because who was Shyanne to take such offense over a man that wasn't hers? It wasn't lost on me how she referred to Xavier without his title, but I wasn't silly enough to think that a man who'd lived for centuries had been alone until he'd found me. But still. Something territorial reared its ugly head inside me — for both Xavier and Pia.

And it was on the third breath that I lost touch with reality.

I sank into the kind of white-hot fury that burned away every other emotion and thought I had — distress, confusion, doubt, relief at having even a partial explanation of what happened to Xavier. All I could focus on was the way Shyanne's face morphed into that of a serpent — her pupils elongating, her tongue forking, her teeth merging into two single points as she held Pia down and hissed in her face. Her freckles turned to pale green scales, and her fingernails grew into claws.

She looked like a genuine monster now, and that made it so easy to unclasp my stythe. I couldn't extend it fully, but there was enough room for me to swing the pommel end against the side of her temple like a club.

Shyanne screamed as she fell off Pia, who remained on the ground, wailing and sobbing and choking as she turned on her side and curled into herself. She covered her ears with her hands in a futile attempt to block out the world, and I stepped between her and Shyanne, who was already picking herself up off the ground.

Instead of waiting for her to regain her bearings though, I gave her a swift kick to the abdomen while she was still down. She grunted and fell back against the wall, and I placed my foot on her chest to hold her there while leveling the sharp end of Mandy against her neck. I couldn't fully extend the weapon, but I didn't need to for my intentions to be clear.

Shyanne sucked in a sharp breath before hissing and glaring up at me with a fresh rage of her own.

"You had a weapon on you?"

"Keep your hands off the girl," I stated, surprising myself with how calm and even my voice sounded. It was monotone and hinted at none of the unbridled anger that was fueling me.

"Watch your own moons!" Shyanne spat.

Her phrasing was unfamiliar to me, but I didn't need the translator to make sense of the meaning behind them. I knew when I was being told to get lost and I met her angry glare with a cold stare of my own.

"If you go near her again," I said, pressing the blade closer until Shyanne hissed and a thin trail of her slick red blood slid across my blade, "I'll kill you."

"You're defending her?" Shyanne asked. "That girl just said she's responsible for Zay's death! She's a murderer!"

"She is not the one who killed him."

"She admitted to it!" Shyanne shouted, jabbing a finger at Pia.

"Howard Wright is the man who killed Xavier. And he's dead now."

"And how would you know that?"

"Because I'm the one who cut off his head," I stated.

"Then what in Jisha's name is she talking about?"

"I plan to find out."

Shyanne stared at me for a moment before slowly lifting her hands up, palms facing forward in the universal sign of surrender. Her gaze was still hostile, but her features morphed back into that of the beautiful, freckle-faced, hazel-eyed woman.

"I'll play nice with the jeiya."

"Good," I said, removing my blade from her neck and my foot from her chest. I took a half-step back, but not enough to give her any real space to move. "But I have a few questions for you first."

"Curious now, are we?" she asked, smirking. "Maybe *you* should've played nice with *me*, aija."

"How did you know Xavier?" I asked, ignoring her taunts.

"Jealous?"

"Murderous, actually," I said, lifting the blade back towards her. "Talk."

"You wouldn't kill a KUAF commander."

"I absolutely would," I said, holding her gaze as I pressed closer. "Your title means nothing to me."

Her hazel eyes darted over to Pia. I don't know what she saw behind me, but it was enough to make her draw back. Her gaze sharpened into a glare, and her words were huskier. She sounded like more beast than woman, and the tone suited her more than the honeyed drawl she'd used before.

"Zay and I were lovers," she stated. "Back when we were both still young."

I nodded.

I'd figured that much.

"And?" I asked. "That doesn't explain why you attacked Pia."

"Anyone would be incensed after what she said."

"Yours wasn't the reaction of some ex-girlfriend," I stated.

"I was more than that to him."

"Are you sure?" I asked, lifting a brow at her. "Cause he never mentioned you once."

"You think he told you everything?" She scoffed and let her eyes dance over me, and I resisted the urge to swing my stythe across her face. "How… simple of you."

"Then how about you tell me what he didn't?"

"I'm sure he had his reasons for not telling you about me, aija," she said, glancing away from me. "You should respect them. Trust me… there are some things you're better off not knowing."

She was probably right, but I couldn't walk away.

Not now.

Not without knowing.

"Unfortunately, I'm not a trusting woman and dead men can't change their minds," I said, drawing her attention back to me. "So, answer the question. Who were you to him, Shyanne?"

"I'm the mother of his child."

5 HOURS

A CAPTIVE

Shyanne's words stopped my world.

Child?

Xavier's child?

My husband had a child, and he didn't tell me about them?

My brain couldn't wrap itself around that. I tried, but every time it was like slamming my skull into a brick wall. I could barely remember how to think — how to breathe. I shook my head and took a step back from Shyanne.

I wanted to deny what she'd said but calling her a liar wouldn't make her one. And Xavier wasn't here to defend himself.

I should've listened when she said I was better off not knowing. My head pounded harder. My vision blurred. My thoughts were rioting and out of control.

A child?

"You're a liar," I whispered.

"Yes, but on this matter, I speak nothing but the truth."

"Zay told me that he didn't have any kids."

"And he didn't," Shyanne said, shrugging. "Not that he knew of, anyway."

"You —"

"Look aija," Shyanne said, cutting me off, "I don't have to explain myself to you or anyone else. But you were his wife, so I'll give you this much…" she shook her head. "Zay is…" she paused and sighed, "*was* a good man. If he told you any lies, he didn't know he was telling them."

Was she really trying to comfort me after that bombshell?

Why?

What was her game here?

"Why are you here?" I asked, glaring at her as I shook my head. "Us meeting like this can't be some random alignment of the stars." Her eyes flicked over to Pia, and I stepped between them. "Don't look at her. I'm the one talking to you right now."

"As I said," she replied, smirking, "I don't have to explain myself to you. All you need to know is that you're slithering through the wrong grass. I'm here for work, and no other reason. So, take care not to make me your enemy while you're here."

"Work?"

I wanted to press her for more answers, but the footsteps pounding outside cut our conversation short. They were heavy, steady, and vibrated the whole room. I glanced toward the door and Shyanne laughed, daring to push against Mandy's blade. It cut into her hand and blood trickled down her arm as she grinned at me.

"Time to put that away, aija," she said, grinning as her eyes morphed back into slits.

"Fine. But I'm not done with you," I shot back, shrinking Mandy down and slapping it onto my wrist as I stepped back to my side of the cell with Pia.

"I'm so scared," she said, chuckling as her forked tongue licked at the blood trailing down her arm. "But I'm not the one you should be keeping an eye on." Her gaze flicked over to where Pia was once more. I couldn't figure out what Shyanne's obsession with her was, but there was no time left to ask.

"Line up," a voice growled from the other side of the door. "It's feeding time."

We were standing shoulder to shoulder when the croc I assumed to be Zoek entered our holding cell. She carried a tray of gray slop, and three filthy mugs filled with murky water. I hadn't expected to receive five-star service, but dying of dysentery wasn't on my bingo card either.

I eyed Zoek as she placed the mugs on the ground in front of us and tried to delude myself into believing I could take her in a fight, but she stood a head taller than all of us. She had to squat down and duck her head to even fit through the door and step into our small cell. Tall as she was though, she was still smaller than the other crocs I'd seen — more delicate.

Her claws were manicured — filed down to smooth, tapered points with glittering silver polish coating the top of them — and her fingers were decorated with rings. The color of her nails and jewelry matched the dusting of silver shadow above her shiny black eyes. Even the tactical jumpsuit she wore was the shimmering color of stardust rather than the saturated blues I'd seen the other crocs wearing. Against her pitch-black scales, Zoek looked oddly majestic as she squeezed her way into our holding cell. She carried herself with a subtle elegance that made it obvious that she wasn't like the rest of the crocs we'd dealt with so far.

Whoever Zoek was, she wasn't a warrior.

The way she took the time to twist the handle of the mugs toward us and place tiny spoons beside each bowl of slop demonstrated a level of kindness that was unwarranted and misplaced among enemies. I hadn't expected Zoek to be so thoughtful, and it was easy to see how Shyanne had sweet-talked her into giving up a wash capsule. Nothing about Zoek was hostile. She seemed like one of the most peaceful beings I'd met since leaving Earth, and for a fraction of a second, I dared to hold out hope that we could talk things out. It was ridiculous, but part of me wanted to believe that we could reason with Zoek and convince her to let us go.

It was a fleeting thought, and before it had any time to take root, Shyanne was breaking rank. She morphed back into the slithering reptile she truly was and launched herself at Zoek as if she had a personal vendetta against her. And maybe she did? Shyanne had been here far longer than we had, and it wouldn't surprise me if a single wash capsule wasn't enough to bridge the gaping rift between Shyanne and the crocs.

So, I watched as Shyanne's hands and feet melted into the rest of her body, and she wrapped herself around Zoek. She constricted her body, squeezing the croc with every muscle she had in an attempt to put out the light in Zoek's eyes.

Zoek let out a shocked screech as she fought back against the sudden attack, clutching at her throat in a desperate bid to free herself — but Shyanne was relentless. She did everything she could to tighten her grip around Zoek even further, but Zoek wasn't some defenseless damsel. Her silver claws dug into Shyanne's body, and she screamed as Zoek ripped through her pale green scales as if they were no stronger than wet paper.

Shyanne aimed her fangs at Zoek's back, but her jumpsuit was more durable than it looked and Shyanne's teeth couldn't even pull a thread loose, let alone do damage. Zoek didn't even flinch from the attempted bite. Instead, she yanked Shyanne from her shoulders and flung her across the tiny room, and for the briefest moment I wondered if I should try to help her.

I quickly decided against that when Shyanne crashed into the wall behind us. She crumpled to the ground in the most dramatic spiral I'd ever seen, and I knew I wouldn't survive a blow like that — not with the way my head was still pounding from the ride over here. Shyanne slumped onto the floor as lines of crimson trickled down her face and glistened against her scales. Her forked tongue flicked out to lick at the stream trailing over her left eye, and she bared her fangs as she pulled herself off the ground. She reared her head back as if she meant to launch herself at Zoek again, but there wasn't enough time.

Glupin beat her to the punch.

I'd forgotten he was with me until he squished out of my right pocket, slipped down my leg, and became a tiny flamethrower on the top of my boot.

I nearly jumped out of my skin when I'd felt him sloshing down my limbs, but the relief I felt at seeing him and knowing he was okay was replaced with slack-jawed shock as he hiccupped a cute little glub before spewing flames across the room.

Zoek tried to avoid them, but the room was too small and she was too big. In an instant she was caught up in his fiery wall, and though her suit protected her, her head, hands and feet were all exposed. She screamed, but it wasn't out of fear.

The sound she emitted was absolutely manic.

Rather than concerning herself with putting out the fire, she dove headfirst toward us, and Shyanne took the opportunity to fling herself at the croc once more. Glupin's flames had already died down, but Shyanne laughed as they spread from Zoek to her and licked at her body. It didn't deter her in the slightest. Instead, she wrapped herself around Zoek's throat and sank her fangs into the side of her face.

They both screeched and hissed and stumbled around the room, smearing blood against the walls and kicking over the trays of slop that had been left on the ground. Zoek slammed her body into the steel walls surrounding us, but it was a wasted effort — there was no way she'd be able to shake Shyanne off her now. Zoek would have to kill Shyanne or rip a chunk of her own face off to pull the serpent-woman away.

It was clear she wasn't sure which route she wanted to take, and I kept my eyes trained on her as she stumbled in our direction. The moment she was away from the door, I snatched Glupin up from my boot and shoved Pia toward the exit. Her violet gaze had been so locked on the fight, she was about to miss the best opportunity we had to escape, and I couldn't allow that. I'd tried to catch her attention a few times before I was half-tackling her out the door, but she'd been oblivious, and the time for gawking was over. With all the noise those two were making, it would only be a matter of time before someone else — someone bigger and stronger — came barging in to put a stop to things and force us back into our place.

"Let's go!"

6 HOURS

A CAPTIVE

Every alarm on the ship blared as the lights flashed red.

I hadn't expected our escape to go unnoticed, but I wasn't prepared for the entire ship to be put on alert the second we stepped outside of our cell. I glanced down the hallway in both directions and tried to make sense of where we were, but it was a struggle.

I'd always hated every kind of strobe light and effect — no matter what I did, it left me feeling like I was moving in slow motion. Under normal circumstances, I could tolerate it, but with the constant ache in my head and blooming pressure behind my eyes, I could barely tell up from down. It felt like the ship was spinning, and I braced myself with a hand against the wall and closed my eyes. I sucked down two deep breaths, but we didn't have time for me to catch my bearings.

"Lady Kyra, are you okay?"

Pia was shouting over the noise, and I forced myself to nod. This wasn't the time for me to fall apart — not when crocs were searching for us, and not when I could see our window of opportunity slipping away from us.

"I'm fine," I said, striding down the hall. I didn't look back to see if she was following behind me, but I trusted that she had enough sense to stick close.

The Croceria was a maze.

Every few feet, there was another hallway branching off into a new direction. Paired with the flashing red lights that disrupted the pitch-black darkness like flashes of lightning, it was disorienting. I couldn't tell how fast we were moving, how far we'd gone, or where we were going, and it didn't help that the air on this ship was thick, like walking through a swamp. It was hot, damp, and muggy. It made breathing far more difficult than it needed to be, and the sweat crawling down my back did nothing to ease my growing panic as Pia and I wove our way through the halls.

"Where are we going?"

I wish I knew.

But her guess was as good as mine.

We were moving, but that was only plan I had for us — keep putting one foot in front of the other. And, as good as that plan was, it would only last us for so long.

We'd be found sooner or later.

In truth, it was a miracle we hadn't been found already, and I didn't want to keep pressing our luck. We needed a place to catch our breath and make a plan, but this ship might as well have been a labyrinth, and I, quite literally, couldn't think straight to save my life. The more we walked, the cloudier my mind got, and I tripped over my own feet more than once and had to brace myself against the wall.

"Are you okay?" Pia asked, reaching out to press her hands against my back. "Maybe we should —"

Her words were cut off by heavy footsteps pounding down the hallway. She gasped, and I gripped her hand before I took off running. I wobbled, but we were out of time.

We had to *move*.

We'd barely taken five steps when I crashed face first into what could only be a wall.

I grunted and staggered backwards into Pia, lifting a hand to my nose as a light clicked on above us. It was a dim white light, but it was sudden and more than enough to blind us as we were ripped from the depths of the dark. I shielded my eyes from it, and before I could do anything to defend myself, my arm was being yanked from my face and twisted behind my back. I hissed as the person who grabbed me shoved me toward the nearest wall with their scaly hand.

I couldn't shake them off.

The croc's grip was like iron, and I groaned at the sharp pain radiating up my arm, but Sigurd had trained me for this moment.

Even with panic clogging my throat and my head spinning, my muscles had been trained to the point where my body moved without my input. I moved my leg behind my attacker, threw my elbow back to hook it over their shoulder, and used their momentum to spin out of the hold and shove them aside. It was obvious they weren't expecting me to be able to defend against them, but there wasn't time for me to appreciate that small win.

Adrenaline was pouring into my system.

I was on autopilot.

I snatched Pia by the hand and took off into the dark.

The croc followed, and soon their footsteps weren't the only ones pounding after us.

We took as many turns as we could.

Left.

Right.

Left.

Right.

Left.

Right.

Left.

Left.

Nothing worked.

We couldn't shake them.

We were faster, but this was their ship. They knew where these hallways led, and we couldn't run forever. That much was obvious. I was already out of breath.

And about to puke.

I had to stop.

I pressed my back against the cold steel of the wall and fought to keep from throwing up my guts right then and there. Pia was huffing too, but she was young — I was the one slowing us down.

"Are you going to make it?" she asked, her violet eyes darting down the hall.

"I'll be fine," I said, wheezing as I pushed off the wall. "Let's keep —"

The wall gave way beneath me.

The world seemed to move in slow motion as I fell backward. Pia's eyes widened as she reached for me. She gripped my hand, but my momentum was too much, and she fell with me.

We landed with a thud on the ground, and I heaved as Pia landed on top of me, and what little air remained in my lungs was knocked out of them. My chest was on fire, and I coughed as I shoved her off me and looked around. I'd been desperate to find someplace — anyplace — to catch our breath, and we'd quite literally stumbled into one.

I was grateful.

Pia collected herself before I did and scrambled over to the door to shut it behind us. It released a soft hiss as it slid shut and plunged us back into absolute darkness. It was unsettling at first, but it was a welcome reprieve from the flashing red lights outside, and relief flooded through me at the realization we'd gotten away.

At least, for now.

"Are you okay?" I asked, whispering into the dark.

"I'm fine," she whispered back. "You?"

"Never better," I muttered, pushing myself up until I was sitting cross-legged on the ground. "You see Glupin?"

As if he heard my question, the little slime lit up, washing the room in a faded yellow light. It created more shadows than anything else, but it was comforting to be able to see again, and I smiled at him. He sat on the ground between Pia and me in a tiny storage room. The walls were lined with shelves weighed down by all kinds of nameless junk, but we were alone, and that's what mattered. Glupin gave a soft little glub, as if he was reassuring me he was still with me, and I patted the top of his squishy little head.

"Did you know he could do that?" Pia asked, wonder in her voice.

"No, but I'm glad he can," I said, grinning down at him. "Good job, Glupin!"

"Yeah," Pia agreed, petting him too. "Good job, buddy."

Silence followed, and I took the moment to collect myself. My head was still spinning, but I could at least ride my own train of thought as I contemplated our situation. A large part of me wanted to interrogate Pia about what she'd said earlier — about it being her fault Xavier was dead. This wasn't the time to focus on that, though. I knew that. What we needed was a way off this ship and back to *The Reveler*. But when I tried to suffocate the thought, rather than going limp and resting in the back of my brain, it fought back. It dug its teeth into me and clawed its way up the back of my throat until it was clear that I was no longer in control.

I was a prisoner to my desperate need for answers.

"Earlier, you said you were the reason Xavier was killed," I said, the words spilling from my mouth with no tact as my brown eyes bore into Pia's violet ones. "I'm going to need you to elaborate on that."

She bit her lip, and I saw it tremble. Her eyes welled with tears, and she blinked countless times trying to hold them back. And when she finally did speak, her voice was hoarse and shaky.

"Because... I *am* the reason Captain Zay..." she paused to suck down a deep breath and clear her throat. "I'm the reason he's dead."

"Why do you feel like Xavier's death is your fault, Pia?"

"Because he died protecting me."

I listened in silence as Pia told me how Xavier died. It was like she held my lungs inside her calloused hands and was squeezing the air out of them with every word, but I kept my face still and just… listened. This wasn't a moment I wanted to relive — I'd endured it the first time when James had shown up on my doorstep with bleary eyes and a galaxy of regret because I'd had to — but this time was different. This pain wasn't new anymore.

I knew how this story ended.

I'd give up any and everything to change it, but time was finite, no matter where in the universe you were. I could beg and plead and bargain with God every day for the rest of my life, and nothing would change. I would still be here, Xavier would still be gone, and this story would still be the end of his.

I didn't want to hear it again.

But it was more important for Pia to get the words out than it was for me to not be hurt by them, so I let her carve a hole into my heart and pour her pain into it.

This story always started the same — on Canaam.

It was a pale green planet on the outskirts of the Milky Way that specialized in body modifications. Nearly everyone there had given up some part of their organic body for technologically improved parts at some point, and it was such an integral part of their culture that it made their planet one of the best places to shop around for improvements.

Sigurd wasn't the only cyborg on *The Reveler*'s crew, so they visited planets like that whenever they could for maintenance and upgrades. When they were in the stars, Chise was the one who piecemealed them together, but she was an engineer, not a doctor. She could tighten a joint or replace an eye, but her bedside manner left a lot to be desired, and there was really no comparing her skill to that of a licensed mechanical surgeon.

So, it hadn't been a big deal for them to stop by Canaam. They'd visited the planet for the first time years ago, on their first trip through the Milky Way. It's how they'd stumbled upon Star Prime 1307 — the tiny blue planet I'd called home. They'd been looking for a place to take a quick vacation after their last job, and Earth was only a three-day trip from Canaam. It was such an unassuming series of events, but it was never lost on me that the same planet that had brought Xavier to Earth had been the same planet that ripped him away from me, but I'd grown used to living with that bittersweet reality.

And this was Pia's story — not mine.

It started with Sigurd.

He'd upped the number of training sessions for the crew and had packed on some fresh muscle in the process. He needed new modifications in his shoulders and elbows to support the added bulk and weight, so they'd gone to Canaam for upgrades, and Pia had disembarked with them.

She'd explored the planet before with the crew, but she usually stayed on the ship since she was too young to wander around on her own. She didn't mind tagging along with Chise when she wasn't going gambling, but Pia wasn't a little girl anymore — she was old enough that hanging out with Sigurd, James, and Xavier wasn't fun for her anymore. In general, she preferred the quiet solitude that came with being one of the only people left on the ship since her idea of a good time was holing up in her room to work on her projects uninterrupted.

She'd been in the middle of developing new weapons for the crew when they returned to Canaam, and she knew they sold a lot more than body modifications. They'd been to the planet countless times over the decade and change they'd spent based on Earth, and Pia was no stranger to Canaam's market — she'd browsed it plenty of times over the years with Chise, and she knew exactly what part she'd needed. So, when Xavier offered to escort her around, she'd hoped it would be a quick trip to buy what she needed and then get back to the ship.

No one could've guessed how everything would fall apart from there.

"I shouldn't have gone," Pia whispered, sniffling and swiping at her eyes as she glared at the floor. "I should've just sent a list or something with Sigurd but…"

"You didn't know what would happen," I said, trying to keep my voice from betraying the way my heart was breaking — both for me and for her. "You went to the market and then what?"

"And then a merchant behind the stall started acting weird," she said, shrugging. "The man restocking the wares kept staring at me, but there were so many people out, I convinced myself that he was just watching the crowd, you know? I tried not to think anything of it, and Captain

Zay didn't say anything either, so I thought it was fine. It wasn't until the merchant behind the stall came over to us that I realized something was seriously off."

"How so?"

"The woman running things kept complimenting me," she said. "Like, she wouldn't stop talking about how pretty my eyes were and how her daughter would love a pair like mine." She shivered at the memory, and I could only imagine how it would feel to have someone look at you as parts to be sold to the highest bidder. "She kept asking me where I got them from, and when I insisted that they were *my eyes*, you know, she changed."

The story only got creepier from there.

The woman tried to cut a deal with Pia for her eyes — offering all types of expensive parts and modifications if she would agree to part with her violet eyes. She wanted to gift them to her daughter and even offered to pay for the surgery and a new pair of cybernetic eyes in any color Pia wanted. When she declined, the woman refused to sell anything to her at all and insisted they wait while she called her partner over to talk to her, convinced that they would be able to change her mind.

"I was too stunned to move, but Captain Zay wasn't having any of that. As soon as she turned her back, he grabbed me by the arm, and we left."

Pia hadn't thought anything more about it, but in a world where body parts are constantly sold and switched out, she'd placed a target on her back by telling the woman in an open market that she still had her natural born eyes.

And had her eyes been brown or blue or gray or green, it wouldn't have been a problem. Canaam's market saw thousands of travelers from just as many planets walk through it every cycle, but none of them had violet eyes — not like hers. With their color, Pia's eyes were considered rare — organic. They would be worth a fortune on the white market, and had she wanted to part with them, that would've been great. But considering that she wanted to leave the planet with them still in her head, it made everything more difficult.

"We'd met back up with Sigurd and James on our way back to the ship, so we thought it would be fine, you know? The three of them were kind of intimidating together."

I could imagine that. I'd never seen them together, but I knew them individually, and all three of them were tall, muscular, dark-skinned, and bald-headed. They walked with confidence, and it seemed that was a psychological weapon to be wielded on any planet. They were men who carried the scars of their previous battles without shame and weren't afraid to start a fight — or end one.

"We were headed back to the ship when Sigurd mentioned that we were being followed," she whispered, her voice getting thick as her version of events began to realign with the version I knew. "They didn't think anything of it because they're them, you know? But body snatchers are a really big thing on planets that do mods, and I tried to stay calm like they were, but I was so scared." Pia wrapped her arms around herself. "I knew what they'd done to Sigurd, and I just…"

"I get it," I said, nodding.

"Sigurd told you what happened to him?" she asked, lifting her gaze to mine. When I nodded again, her violet eyes grew wide. "I'm surprised. Chise is the one who told me because he never talks about himself."

I chose not to argue with her. Sigurd wasn't a chatterbox, but he wasn't a vault either. He just wasn't the type to volunteer information. But maybe that's just how he was with me? I had no idea how he was around other people, so I couldn't tell whether Pia just never took an interest in Sigurd or if he was purposeful in shutting her out.

"He told me. And I understand why that would scare you. But how does Xavier tie into this?"

"He was the one who saved me from getting shot," she answered, tears streaking down her round cheeks at the memory. "The body snatchers had followed us from the market and told the three of them to hand me over. All of them were armed but..." she paused as she lifted her head and a tiny smile brushed across her lips. "Captain Zay told them to go pawn themselves and shot the leader." She cleared her throat as she wiped the tears from her cheeks. "It's not that interesting when I tell the story, but Captain Zay was so cool. He took out three of them before anyone could move. And then James was shoving me at Sigurd and we were running away," she said, her voice dropping again. "I couldn't tell what was happening," she admitted. "People were screaming and running everywhere, and it was so crowded... I couldn't keep up with Sigurd. He was basically just dragging me behind him and shoving people out the way. James and Captain Zay were right behind us, covering our backs, but I kept slowing them down, and then..."

She sobbed as she looked away from me.

I knew this part of the story.

My throat burned, but I waited for her to get the words out.

"There was… someone aiming for me," she whispered. "I felt the scope on my back. It was so hot…" she said, shaking her head. "Sigurd told me to duck, but I didn't… I couldn't understand what he was saying and… everything was so loud…" she swiped at her eyes and sniffled and buried her face in her hands. "Captain Zay was the one who pushed me out of the way. And it was like, everything just stopped, you know? I couldn't breathe."

That, I very much understood.

It was hard to breathe now, and it had been months since I'd had to hear this same story from James — months since I'd had to bury Xavier on Earth.

"Captain Zay took the hit and told us to run. Told James and Sigurd to protect me," she said, her voice getting smaller with each word. "I didn't want to leave but…"

"You ran away," I said, finishing the story. "Sigurd took you back to the ship."

"I never… saw… Captain Zay… again," she sobbed. "I shouldn't… have run… I shouldn't… have been there!"

"You did what you were told to do," I said, keeping my words soft. "You did the right thing Pia."

"I should've stayed!"

"The only thing that would've changed if you had is that you would've died too," I said, shaking my head.

"But Captain Zay —"

"Died protecting you," I said, my own voice growing thick as my throat burned with every emotion I couldn't let go of.

This was why James had refused to tell me how someone as weak as Howard Wright had gotten the drop on Xavier. It wasn't because he'd outsmarted them — it was because Xavier had sacrificed himself for the girl sitting across from me.

The girl I'd befriended.

The girl he didn't want me to resent.

"Don't make his sacrifice worthless by saying you should've disobeyed his direct order to run away or that you should've been the one who died instead," I warned. "I'll never forgive you if you disrespect his memory like that." She snapped her mouth shut, and I sucked in a shaky breath. "It's not your fault that he died, Pia."

Those words were so hard to choke out.

Because part of me wanted to blame her.

Part of me wanted *someone* to be mad at — to have a target to throw all of this sadness and empty rage at. But this wasn't Pia's burden to carry. Xavier's death had nothing to do with her — she was just in the wrong place at the wrong time, and this wasn't her guilt to carry. It was stupid and selfish and insane, but it didn't feel right to have anyone else hurt more than I did.

All the anger and guilt over Xavier's death was *mine*.

This was the pain I'd laid claim to and the pain that fueled me, that pushed me forward. She was too young to hold onto that kind of heartbreak, and I narrowed my eyes at her. I was fighting back my own unshed tears, but I blinked them away.

I wasn't going to let her keep this grief.

"Xavier died because someone wanted him dead," I said, meeting her gaze. "That man you saw watching you at the stall…" I paused to take a steadying breath and clear my throat. "That man, he had a beard, right? One that didn't meet in the middle? Kinda lanky?"

"How do you…?"

"That was Howard Wright," I said, biting off the end of his name. "It might have seemed like a coincidence to you, but everything about that meeting had been manufactured before you guys ever got there."

"But… why?"

"Control," I answered. "Epidemic has been trafficking 'organic materials'," I said, throwing up air quotes around the words, "through the Milky Way for decades. The KUAF doesn't have a base out there, so there was no one to get in his way until you guys came along."

"We took over his transport routes," she whispered, her violet eyes growing to the size of saucers.

"Exactly," I said, nodding. "You guys start moving people and product through legitimate channels, and that cut into Epidemic's profit. Less profit, less power, less control." I swallowed against the frustration clogging the back of my throat as I shook my head. "Xavier's success brought the KUAF's attention to the Milky Way, and Epidemic didn't like that. So, he put a bounty on Zay's head."

"Then that means…"

"You two being targeted that day had nothing to do with you," I said, holding her gaze and doing my best to make sure she actually heard me. "There was nothing you could have done to save him, Pia. Even if you hadn't left the ship that day, they still would have found an excuse to attack him. They just would've targeted someone else in the crew. But Howard Wright would have still pulled the trigger, and I still would have hunted him down and cut off his head."

"But…"

"But nothing," I said, cutting her off as I leaned forward and reached forward to grip her hand. It was ice cold. "Listen to me, Pia. Some things are inevitable. You can't hold yourself responsible for things that were never under your control. Do you understand me?"

"I think so."

"Good," I whispered, releasing her hand and looking away as tears streaked down her face. "Just… appreciate Xavier for protecting you. Don't waste the time he's given you."

"Okay," she whispered, sobbing and nodding. "I can do that."

7 HOURS

A CAPTIVE

Once Pia collected herself, we devised a simple plan: make a beeline for the escape pods, hijack one, and make our way back to *The Reveler*. It was all Pia's idea, and though there were plenty of holes in it — like the fact that the escape pods were probably heavily guarded following our escape, the crocs might not have any on the ship at all, we had no idea where they were or how to get to them, and even with Pia's genius, it would take her some time to reprogram them to our destination — I didn't have a better one.

Not with the five hours we had left.

Pia had been adamant that Sigurd and Chise wouldn't let the ship fly off without us, but I didn't have her kind of blind, youthful trust in others. So, while she placed all our eggs in the basket of escape, my brain worked overtime to figure out other options.

But every alternative that I thought of involved us taking over the ship.

And while I would've trusted that more if I were with Sigurd or

James or literally anyone else, Pia couldn't fight, I wasn't in the best shape, and I held within me no delusions of grandeur. Finding the control center would be easy enough, but I wouldn't be able to take command of it on my own. So, we decided to go with Pia's plan.

She was a mechanic for *The Reveler* and had spent more time on spaceships than off them, so her innate sense of direction on *The Croceria* was better than mine. She swore up and down that she could lead us to where the escape pods were, so I decided to trust her.

My faith was tested at first. We were fumbling through the dark hallways, and with the flashing red lights, blaring alarms, and the possibility of an enemy lurking around every corner, my nerves were shot. I was still recovering from Zentrith's oh-so-gentle handling of me during our capture, and the constant twists and turns on this ship weren't helping my mental at all. My head pounded, my body ached, and the more we walked, the closer I came to losing my mind.

All I wanted at this point was a soft bed, a hot shower, a cold pillow, and absolute silence. Instead, what I got was another long, empty stretch of hallway. It felt like the universe was mocking me for putting my faith in a teenager, but before I could grab her attention and suggest we turn back, the lights flashed, and I saw a giant, double-wide door that could only lead to the hangar bay.

Pia had actually done it.

She'd managed to find a way off this ship. All we needed now was to get inside, and it would be smooth sailing from there. A smile flitted across my face as I dared to hope that we were nearing the end of the awful journey, but it was too soon to feel relief. We still needed to be careful —

there was no telling how heavily guarded this area was.

I opened my mouth to say as much to Pia, but she was already rushing forward, taking bold steps toward our demise. I reached for her hand — shirt — elbow — anything I could grab to drag her back, but she was tiny and fast. By the time I registered the fact that she was moving away from me, she was out of reach, and I was reminded, once again, that no matter how reliable she was, Pia was still just a reckless kid.

I didn't even have time to call her name before the double doors slid open, and a croc stepped out, locking eyes with us as he banged his fist against the nearest wall, drawing the attention of every other croc nearby.

"There they are!"

The voice of an angry croc was the last thing I wanted to hear, but I didn't have time to waste on being annoyed. Instead, I darted forward and snatched Pia back. There would be no getting away this time, but I was better prepared this time when the crocs threw a blinding white spotlight on us. I closed my eyes and shoved Pia behind me as I whipped out Mandy and extended the blade. My eyes adjusted quickly, and I was met with the light of three green lasers being trained on us.

I dared to let myself feel a little relief that they didn't shoot us on sight. It confirmed one thing for certain: they wanted us alive.

For what reason, I couldn't say, but I was going to make the most of the opportunity.

Every muscle in my body ached, and the pounding in my skull only increased with the fresh wave of adrenaline pouring into my system. Panic tightened my chest, and I tried to disentangle myself from it, but the harder I tried, the deeper I sank into it until my heart was in my throat and I couldn't make sense of my own thoughts.

My stythe wouldn't do much against lasers, but it was something. I held my arm out in front of Pia to protect her, but to her credit, she had her fists balled up and in front of her face as if she could take one of the crocs in a fight.

"Stay behind me," I whispered. "And run the second you get a chance to."

"I'm not leaving you."

I glared down at her. This was not the time for her to be a stubborn teenager.

"Throw down your weapon!"

Who in their right mind would do that?

My palms grew slick with sweat as I stared into the blinding light. I squinted, trying to make out who was on the other side — how many crocs had cornered us. Just because there were only three lasers trained on us now didn't mean there weren't more waiting in the shadows, and I blinked, willing my eyes to adjust to the brightness.

But everything was just white and red and flashing.

"Lady Kyra, on your left!"

Pia sounded like she was a million miles away, so I was grateful when Glupin blew fire at the attackers.

For the second time in as many hours, I'd forgotten about my little slime buddy, and for a half-second, my stomach dropped with guilt. It was fleeting, but as Glupin squished his little head out of my pocket, I made a mental note to let him float in the warmest bath and feed him a whole pack of matches when we made it back to *The Reveler*. He'd come to my rescue more than once and was proving himself to be the MVP of this escape mission.

The crocs growled and swatted at the unexpected flames, and though I couldn't see them, I swung my stythe in their general direction. It didn't do much, but I could hear them grunt as they jumped back.

I gripped Pia's arm and flung her toward an empty hallway shrouded in darkness and smoke.

"Run!"

"But —"

"I'm right behind you!"

She hesitated for a moment before she sprinted away.

I held my left hand out to Glupin and let him squish around my fist. It was like immersing my hand in hot jello. It was an odd sensation, but it grounded me. I held him out to the crocs who were starting to force their way through the dwindling flames and shouted at him.

"Glupin, use flamethrower!"

He glubbed and spewed out another wall of flames. It was hotter than the first time, and even I had to take several steps back. I stood in awe for a moment before seizing the opportunity Glupin had created for me.

I turned on my heel and sprinted around the corner, after Pia.

The world was still spinning and began to blur around the edges, but I forced my feet forward. I needed to find Pia — to find a way off this ship — to figure out if Shyanne was telling the truth — to get back to *The Reveler*.

To find Xavier's child.

There was so much to be done, but it was so, *so* hard to breathe.

I doubled over and placed a hand to my chest.

I gasped for breath.

A sob broke through.

No.

No.

I gritted my teeth, shook my head, and forced myself forward.

This wasn't the time or the place to feel things.

To feel anything.

And I'd feed myself to the crocs before I broke down in tears here.

But the more I tried to ignore things — to shove down every doubt and fear and keep going, the harder it got to breathe. To think. To focus. To move. My head pounded harder, and the pressure behind my eyes kept growing until my vision was jumping with every pulse.

I had to stop.

I was exhausted.

"You need to get out of here," I whispered to Glupin, knowing full well he wouldn't be like Pia. I wasn't going to be able to shove him into the darkness with the expectation he'd keep going without me. "They're going to find us."

He made a tiny glub as if he understood.

As if to say that he didn't care.

He gave a little vibrating glub as he climbed up to my shoulder and lifted his little slime body up to squish his head to the side of my face — and I couldn't tell if it was because I was desperate, depressed, or concussed, but it truly felt as if Glupin was doing his best to comfort me.

And that just made me want to cry more.

"Thanks, Glupin," I whispered, letting my eyes drift closed as footsteps pounded down the hall. "I needed that."

9 HOURS
A CAPTIVE

I hated waking up in the dark.

Always had.

It was one of the reasons I'd always been terrified of going to space with Xavier, though I'd never admitted it — not really. Not to him and not to myself. But I'd always been the kid who'd needed a nightlight. My parents had always left the hallway light on for me just in case I needed to go to the bathroom in the middle of the night, and even as an adult, I'd sprung for the fancy strip lights to line the floorboards of our hallways and beneath our bed. I'd done it under the guise of it being great mood lighting, but honestly and truly, I hated the dark.

It was so loud.

There were no distractions to help me silence the most ruthless parts of my mind.

The parts that reminded me of every mistake I'd ever made.

Every regret.

Every doubt.

Everything I wanted to forget.

The dark made it impossible to forget what Shyanne had said, and I couldn't ignore the very possible reality that she was telling the truth. I didn't want to think about it, but I didn't have a choice. My thoughts latched onto her words and replayed them over and over again on a loop in my mind.

I'm the mother of his child.

I felt like such an idiot, and I couldn't decide if I wanted to laugh or scream or cry.

I'd known that Xavier had kept his secrets — I'd kept a few of my own — but I never imagined anything like this.

A child.

Had he really not known?

I had no reason to trust Shyanne, but who would lie about something like this?

Maybe she was lying about even knowing Xavier?

I could ask James. He probably knew the truth.

The pit of my stomach fell out with that thought.

Yeah… he *definitely* knew. Which meant that Sigurd probably did too. Honestly, the entire crew probably knew about Shyanne Olight and her relationship with Xavier, and my stomach twisted at that. There I was, walking around as his wife — his visibly distraught widow — trying to figure out how to go on without him and live up to the role of captain, and he had a child out there somewhere by another woman.

I felt like such a clown. I might as well have put the red nose on myself.

I sighed and pressed my hands to my face.

What if Xavier's child...

I shook my head and sucked down a deep breath. Held it. Waited until my lungs ached before blowing it out.

This was not the time to ponder what-ifs. That would only lead me back into the all-consuming depression I'd just clawed my way out of. I couldn't afford to go back to that place — to face all the emotions that were waiting for me there.

This was not the time to cry.

I was still surrounded by crocs with no idea how to escape.

I had to focus.

"Lady Kyra?"

I bolted upright at the sound of my name, and my eyes searched the dark.

"Pia?"

As if on cue, Glupin glubbed next to me before emitting his soft light. It pushed back the dark like the tiny lights my parents had plugged into the corner of my room at night, and I scanned the shadows, searching for a familiar face as I scooped him into my arms. He was like a tiny space heater in my hands, chasing away the chill that crept over me as I realized that I was back in a holding cell with Pia. Although, this one was significantly nicer than the last one we'd been thrown into, and that didn't make sense to me.

Why would they show us more kindness after we'd tried to escape?

It made me suspicious of the bed I sat on. It was covered in soft sheets with a thick blanket folded neatly at the foot of the bed. The walls and floors were still made out of what I could only guess to be the space version of concrete, but there was a small table next to the bed with a stack of books in a language I couldn't read, and a short couch on the other side of the room that Pia was on. Her knees were pulled to her chest, and her shoulders sank with relief when I swung my legs over the edge of the bed.

"You're awake," she whispered.

"How long was I out?" I asked, looking around. "Where are we?"

"About two hours, according to my count," she answered. "And we're in the captain's quarters."

I froze.

"What?" I shook my head and hissed as a sharp pang rang through my head. I placed a hand on my forehead and took a deep breath. "Why?"

"I don't know," she said, shrugging. "This is just where they dragged us to. But I saw the sign by the door. This is definitely the captain's room."

I sighed and tried to keep calm as my mind raced to piece together a very scattered puzzle.

"Explain to me how we ended up here together," I said, lifting my gaze to hers. "You weren't anywhere around when I…"

I let my words trail off, but we both knew what had happened. I'd passed out in the middle of the hallway during our escape plan while on an enemy ship — and if that wasn't the dumbest thing I'd ever done, it was for sure in the top three. It was embarrassing to even think about, and I squeezed Glupin tighter as I held her gaze.

"I know why I got caught, but why are you here, Pia? You had a head start."

"I came back for you," she answered, wrapping her arms tighter around herself. "I tried to save you."

"And?" I asked, trying to swallow my frustrations. "What happened?"

"When I found you, you were unconscious. I tried to drag you but…"

"I was too heavy for you," I said, nodding and filling in the gaps she didn't want to say out loud. "I'm almost two hundred pounds of dead weight, so no. You weren't moving me."

"Right."

"Okay," I said, stressing the word and lifting my brows at her. "But you still haven't answered how you got caught with me. Did you not run when you heard the crocs coming?"

"I couldn't just abandon you!"

This girl.

I took a deep breath and set Glupin on the bed next to me so that I could give Pia my full, undivided attention. I braced my elbows on my knees and laced my fingers together between them.

"Pia, did I not tell you to run?"

"Yes, but I…" Her words trailed off as if she expected me to cut her off, but I waited. She wasn't getting off the hook so easily. She would have to find the words to explain herself, and I watched as she scrambled to organize her thoughts. "I waited for you to catch up to me. But when you didn't show, I got worried and doubled back. That's when I saw you and tried to save you."

Save me.

I sighed.

"Okay," I said, trying to rein in all the sharp words that pricked at my tongue. "I understand why you came back," I said, dragging out the words as I searched for the ones that would allow me to safely navigate this conversation riddled with landmines. "After what happened with Zay, I get it. I do," I assured her. "I know it wasn't easy for you to go on without me, but," I said, emphasizing the word when she started to smile at me, "that doesn't excuse the fact that I gave you a direct order and you purposefully disobeyed me."

"I didn't think it was that kind of order," she said, shrinking into herself.

"What kind did you think it was?" I asked, straightening up. "A suggestion?"

"I don't know."

"That's not an answer," I said, frowning. "You're going to have to dig deeper than that."

"But I *don't* know!"

"You're old enough to pay attention to your own thoughts, Pia. So, if you didn't think I was giving 'that kind of order' then stand ten-toes down behind that and tell me what you thought it was."

"I don't know…" when I glared at her she sighed and straightened up. "I guess… I'm just so used to you being chill with me, you know? You've never given me orders like that so…"

"So, you thought they were optional," I finished for her, nodding my head. She didn't move to contradict me, and I could only cough out a laugh at the reality smacking me in the face.

This was my doing.

"I get it, now. Though, I can't blame you," I admitted. "It's not like we met under the best conditions. I was depressed and angry, and to top it off, I'm not some natural born leader with charisma," I said, shrugging. "I didn't act like a captain when I boarded *The Reveler*, and now you don't see me as one."

"That's not true!"

"You don't have to lie to me."

"But it's not true, Lady Kyra," she said, lowering her voice as she shook her head. "It's not."

"So, you're telling me that if Captain Zay had given you a direct order, you would've ignored that one, too?"

She was silent as she dropped her gaze to the ground, and I chided myself for throwing that in her face. It was a low blow. I knew that, but she wasn't the only one hurting here, and I was struggling to keep my own frustrations under control. I sighed and tugged at my afro before trying again to find the right words — softer ones.

"Look, Pia," I said, drawing her gaze back to me. "I shouldn't have said that. But I don't need you to deny the truth for me, okay? The facts are what they are. I wasn't the best captain when I boarded *The Reveler*, and I own that. However," I said, giving her a pointed look as she averted her eyes from mine, "I *am* still the captain. I'm the one in charge, and when I give orders, I expect them to be followed. Even if you don't like them."

"That's not fair."

"Life's not fair, kid."

"So, I'm just supposed to be a good little soldier and fall in line whenever you tell me to?" she asked, her eyes shining with tears as she released her knees and slammed her feet to the floor. "I'm not expected to think for myself?"

"You are always expected to think for yourself," I stated, holding her gaze. "But sometimes thinking for yourself looks like doing exactly what you're told to do. And I expect you to be able to realize when those moments arrive." I shook my head. "You shouldn't have doubled back for me."

"But you said you'd be right behind me," she said, swiping at her eyes as she glared at me. "Maybe if you hadn't lied to me —"

"Lied to you?" I scoffed and bit back a laugh as I ground my teeth to keep from snapping at her. "Pia. We are on an enemy ship, hurtling through space to god-knows-where, as prisoners to a known alien trafficker. Do you understand that?" I asked, pausing to pull in a breath, shaking with suppressed anger. "Because if you do, you should understand why I would send you on without me. You are a *mechanic*, Pia," I reminded her. "You're the only one who can reprogram the escape pods to get us out of here. But if you're captured with me, who's going to reach the ship and send for help?"

I relied on the logic behind my words to reach her, but in truth, I would have told her to run regardless. There was no way I was risking her life to save mine, even if she wasn't a mechanic — even if she was just a normal, average girl, and I could work the escape pods on my own. But Pia wouldn't appreciate that sentiment. Not when Xavier had sacrificed himself for her. She saw herself as far more expendable than I did — like her life somehow mattered less than mine — so I kept that part to myself.

"I didn't think about that," she admitted, dropping her gaze to the floor.

"Of course you didn't," I said, shrugging. "It's not your job to think about stuff like that. It's *mine*. And I did think about it, which is why I told you to run. And you should've run simply because I said so."

Pia didn't say anything, and I have never known silence to be so loud. All she did was glare at the floor as tears dropped from her eyes onto her balled fists, and I stared at the chasm stretching between us.

It would have been easier if I didn't know how we'd gotten on opposite sides of this argument, but I could see every misstep I'd taken to get to this point. I'd trusted her with things too heavy to carry. I chose to rely on her like a friend and treated her like an adult when she was still, very much, a child. I'd allowed her constant presence to lull me into believing she could handle my duality — my grief and my guidance, my hope and my heartbreak — when she'd yet to work through her own.

I shouldn't have let her skip work with me when I needed a shoulder to lean on. I should have reached out to her when she pulled away instead of giving her space to wallow in her misery alone. I'd placed my grief on top of hers and never thought to ask how she was carrying it all.

That would have to change.

Our safety was the priority right now, and every plan was doomed to fail if she tried to 'power of friendship' our way through every problem. I understood why she thought staying with me was a good idea, but I couldn't ignore it either. There were more than fifteen years of experience separating us, and even if this was my first time out in space, it wasn't my first time looking at the big picture to solve a problem.

So, despite the fact that I heard my mother's voice coming out of my mouth — that phrases like *life isn't fair* and *because I said so* felt foreign on my tongue — I met Pia's gaze and said what I had to.

"Listen, Pia," I whispered, lowering my voice as if that would soften the blow of my words. "You don't have to like me or the orders I give, but you will respect them. My job is to make sure you get back to the ship in one piece, and that's what I'm going to do, even if I have to strap you to an escape pod and yeet you into space myself. So, the next time I tell you to do something, do it. Understand?"

"Yes, captain."

"Good," I said, nodding as my heart cracked at the pure betrayal echoing in her words. "Then let's do what we have to, to get out of here."

10 HOURS

A CAPTIVE

Pia's cheeks were still wet when the lock on the door clicked open.

We both jumped to our feet and watched as the lean figure of a tall man filled the doorway. A small orb of light hovered over his head and followed him inside, brightening the room. It completely swallowed Glupin's light, and I scooped him back into my arms.

I don't know what kind of person I'd expected to be confronted with, but it wasn't the welcoming face of a human-looking man. I knew better than to assume he came from the same place I did at this point — Pia, James, Sigurd, and countless other members of *The Reveler* crew could pass as natives from Earth, too — but it was hard to fight the instinctual way I wanted to lower my guard as I stared back into his dark green eyes.

"Calm down," he said, waving his hand at us as he closed the door behind him. "I'm here to talk."

"Talk?" I repeated, backing up to stand between him and Pia.

"Yes," he said, taking a seat on the edge of the bed I'd just vacated.

"Talk. Or did you think there was some other reason I brought you here?"

"You can never trust the intentions of a man who drags a woman to his bedroom against her will."

The man studied me for a moment, surprise flitting across his face before his lips spread wide in a grin, and he barked out a laugh. It was a big sound, full of light and freedom. It didn't match the situation at all and only served to put me further on edge.

"I hadn't realized I made a joke."

"You wouldn't," he said, chuckling under his breath once more. "Rest assured, Lady Kyra. I've never touched a woman in any way she's not desired me to. And I have no designs on you or your little crewmate there," he said, pointing to Pia. "The circumstances may be less than ideal, but my intentions are honest."

I studied the man as I weighed whether or not to believe his words.

He had the kind of square jaw that made it seem as if God had drawn his face with a ruler. His skin was a honeyed shade of light brown, his lips were pink, and the loose curls spilling over the top of his tapered cut were a shade of green that matched his eyes. Two gold earrings glinted in his left ear, and had he not been holding us prisoner — had we not been in space and had we not been captured by his crew — I probably would've found him to be objectively handsome.

But the situation was what it was, and I glared when he smirked at us. His eyes locked onto mine, and while I was grateful he didn't have much interest in Pia, I had to work at quelling the growing desire I had to throw my boot into his groin. His words seemed true enough, but he was far from the kind of person I'd be fool enough to trust. He didn't seem to be lying though, and it wouldn't be wise to make any more of an enemy out of him just yet.

We were still alive, we weren't shackled or separated, and he'd taken the time to arrange a meeting with us. He clearly had a reason for that, and the least I could do was listen to his reasons why.

"Then how about some proper introductions, first?" I asked, holding his gaze and pulling my shoulders back. "It's clear that you know me, but I don't know you. Who do I have the displeasure of speaking with?"

"Drexel C. Barnes," he said, offering me a lopsided grin that probably would've melted most women. "But you can call me Rex. I'm the interim captain of this ship, and you," he said, drumming his long fingers against his knee, "have been causing nothing but stress for my crew."

"Interim?" I repeated, narrowing my eyes. "Where's your actual captain?"

"That's a bit of a long story, actually," he said, as some of the mirth in his grin faded. "I'd be happy to tell you about it, if you could spare me a moment of your time?"

His words were airy and light and easygoing, and nothing about him made sense. He was treating this like some casual encounter when I was literally fighting to escape him with our lives. It was disconcerting how he seemed more like a lazy beach boy than a cruel space captor, and I couldn't fathom how someone like him ended up cornering us on a spaceship like this.

"How do we know you're not going to kill us?" Pia asked.

My eyes shot down to her, and I stifled the urge to sigh and press my palm to my forehead. They'd had plenty of opportunities to kill us already

— on the ship, in transit, in the holding cell, when we escaped the holding cell, when I passed out in the hallway. But not only had they not executed us, we hadn't been harmed in the slightest. There was a reason for that, and Rex confirmed as much when he snorted and rolled his eyes at her.

"If I wanted you dead, you'd be dead already. Or did you think you were being sneaky while you were running around the ship and shouting at each other over the alarms?"

A flutter of embarrassment made heat rise up my neck, and I narrowed my eyes at Rex, but what could I say? He had a point. Even if we had been able to break out of our holding cell and find a decent enough hiding spot, it didn't matter if everyone could hear us. But his logic raised new questions.

"Then why *haven't* you killed us?" I asked. "Seems like it's not worth your trouble to keep us alive."

"And that is where you would be wrong, my dear Kyra," he said, grinning as I glared harder at the way he said my name. "I have my own reasons for doing things."

"And those would be?"

He gestured to the couch. "Sit, and we can talk about it."

I let my eyes graze over him, but his face was unreadable. I couldn't figure out why he would go to such lengths just to have a conversation, especially when he didn't know me. But my options were limited. Even if there were a scenario where Pia and I could overpower him — which was basically an impossible task in and of itself — there was no way we'd make it out of this room or very far beyond it. We'd tried that twice now and had failed miserably each time. So, rather than repeating the same mistake a third time, I took a step back and lowered myself down onto the edge of the seat.

Glupin glubbed in my arms, but he didn't go anywhere. It was like he wanted to make his presence known — either to reassure me or to warn Rex, but it was impossible to tell, and I wasn't convinced I wasn't just making things up. Pia moved to sit next to me, but Rex held up his hand and stopped her.

"Not you," he said, shaking his head. "Wait outside."

"What?" Pia asked, her eyes growing big as saucers as her gaze bounced between me and Rex. "You can't be serious."

"Do you have that much separation anxiety that you can't be without your captain for a few minutes?"

"It's called loyalty," Pia snapped. "I'm not leaving her here alone with you!"

"I promise not to do anything to your captain she doesn't want me to do," he said, winking at her. "But we don't need an audience. Unless your captain's into that?"

He cast a quick glance over to me, and Pia gasped at the implication behind his words. Her violet eyes bounced around the room, landing on everything and seeing nothing, as she balled her fists at her sides and threw intermittent glares at Rex. He tried to swallow his amusement, but he failed and ended up laughing in her face anyway.

Her reaction was a stark reminder that her life didn't extend beyond the work she did. Which made sense — as far as I knew, she spent most of her time with the crew, and they were all adults. There were passengers around her own age on the ship, but she was hardly ever around them.

She definitely wasn't close enough to anyone to have any kind of romantic interest in them.

It made me worry for a moment that being on *The Reveler* wasn't the best thing for her, but that was something I could worry about on a different day. For now, I just placed a hand on her arm. When she turned to me, I offered her a tiny smile.

"It's okay," I told her. "I'll be fine."

I could see the argument brewing in her eyes. Her face flushed, and she opened her mouth, but then she closed it. She snapped it shut and narrowed her violet eyes at me before glancing at Rex and angling her body away from him so that he couldn't see her mouth, as if he wouldn't be able to hear her whisper in this tiny room.

"Are you sure?"

"Positive," I said, nodding and handing her Glupin. "Take him with you. Just in case."

She accepted Glupin with a tiny nod, and he made a little popping sound I'd never heard before. It sounded like crackling fire, and I placed a hand on his head with a smile.

"I'll be fine," I reassured him. "Take care of Pia for me. If anyone tries to come near her," I said, lifting my gaze and letting it lock onto Rex for my next words, "burn them alive."

He chuckled, and when Pia turned back to face him, he stepped over to the door. He opened it and called out a name in the darkness. There was quiet movement, and then a croc that was about my height filled the doorway. She was in the same kind of tactical suit as the others we'd seen before, but her scales were a pale green rather than the dark green ones we'd seen before — and a far cry from the shiny black scales that Zentrith had. I didn't know if it was a sign of age or just an inherited trait, but the light color made her look much younger than the rest of the crocs we'd seen. Her eyes were a bright shade of gold, and she looked as apprehensive as Pia did when they flickered over to us. Rex whispered something to her, and she lifted her hand in a silent wave.

"This is Olexia," Rex said, gesturing to the girl. "She's one of my personal guards, and I promise she won't lay a hand on your…" he paused and considered Pia in silence before shrugging, "person. They'll be just outside the door in the other room, and no one would be bold enough to enter here without permission."

So, we were in an inner room. It wasn't much information, but it confirmed that I'd made the right decision to just talk to Rex. We were, no doubt, surrounded by crocs. So, even if Pia and I had managed to make it past him, we wouldn't have made it far.

"I'm going to hold you to that," I said, nodding.

He returned the gesture and stepped aside as Pia walked over to the door. Olexia looked down at Pia, and though I guessed them to be around the same age, Olexia made Pia's five-two frame seem even smaller than she was. Her wild hair gave her the illusion of some added height, but Pia was truly a tiny girl. I had the irrational desire to tell her to stay, but it was just that — irrational. This wasn't a conversation she needed to be a part of. That much was apparent from the way Rex had orchestrated her departure.

It would've been easy for him to separate us from the start, but he hadn't. It was likely to earn my gratitude in the moment, and despite knowing that, his plan still worked. I'm glad I hadn't woken up alone, especially in his bedroom. I wouldn't have been able to focus on anything but Pia, and whatever conversation he wanted to have with me now wouldn't have happened.

I respected his foresight and had to admit my curiosity was piqued.

Olexia led the way out of the room, and Pia followed behind her. Glupin lit up as they stepped into the dark hallway, and Pia cast a quick glance over her shoulder at me before letting the dark swallow her. Rex shut the door behind them and returned to his seat on the edge of the bed.

We were genuinely alone for the first time, and my shoulders tensed as he leaned forward to rest his arms on his knees. The laissez-faire attitude he'd had before slipped away, and I could see for the first time the steel core of a man used to being in charge and making hard decisions.

"Alright," he said, his voice gaining a new edge to it, "let's get straight to the point. You're here because I need a favor from you."

"And why would I do anything for you?"

"Because you need my help if you're ever going to get off this ship," he stated. "To be blunt, you've only made it this far because I've allowed it. I told Zoek to leave the door to your cell open. I kept the alarms flashing so you could at least see where you were going, and I had my crew chase you toward the storeroom on the third level. Or did you not find it odd that no one on this ship could catch up to you?"

"Why would you help us?"

"Because I need something from you," he said, lacing his fingers together. "And I figured if I shake your hand, you'd shake mine." When I lifted a brow at him in confusion, he frowned. "I was told that was a common Star Prime 1307 saying."

"That's not the issue. I get what you were *trying* to say, but…" I squinted at him. "What do you want from me Drexel?"

"For you to take my sisters off this ship and make them part of your crew."

I lifted my brows at him and waited for the punchline of his joke, but when none came, I realized he was serious. This conversation was taking a turn I hadn't expected, and I studied him as I mulled over his words. Drexel C. Barnes wasn't an easy man to read. His dark green eyes were locked onto me, and his jaw was clenched as he waited for my response. For the first time since meeting him, he seemed… earnest.

"That's a big ask," I stated, lacing my fingers together as I mulled the request over. "Why?"

"The short version of the story?" He shrugged. "I don't want my sisters caught up in the same mess I am. And right now, you're the only person who I know for sure isn't working for Epidemic."

Epidemic.

The man who'd put the hit out on Xavier's life.

His name alone was enough to set my blood on fire.

"What does he have to do with this?"

I stared, unblinking into Rex's green eyes and tried to keep my breathing steady, but every part of my body sang with a desire for pain and destruction. I braced my hands on my knees as I tried to keep them from trembling with rage and sat up straighter.

"Did I step on a nerve?"

"Stomped on a landmine, actually."

"Figures," Rex said, letting a wry smile cross his lips. "That man doesn't know how to make anything but enemies." He shook his head and pulled a hand through his hair as I waited. "I won't bore you with the details of how I ended up here but know that I am a very reluctant employee of his."

"Oh?" I asked, quirking an eyebrow upward.

"Like I said, it's a mess," he said, shaking his head. "But I plan to clean it up. Believe that."

"And if I don't?"

"Doesn't matter. That's not why I'm telling you this."

"Then get to your point," I said, glaring at him.

"My *point* is," he said, stressing the word, "that you killed Howard Wright."

"And?"

"And everyone knew he worked for a supernova like Epidemic. That was the only thing keeping that putrid rodent alive," he said, sucking his teeth. "He was the type of man to bite the hand that fed him, but Epidemic was too dangerous to piss off. It's why he tucked his tail and ran off to Zaigera. But then you..." he said, the smirk I was beginning to associate with him spilling across his face again. "You came in and cut his head off in broad daylight. It was like you declared war on Epidemic and didn't care.

Didn't even flinch at the idea."

He looked at me with his green eyes full of expectation and something I could only guess to be awe — or maybe respect? Either way, I had no use for his validation and shrugged. I hadn't done it to impress him or anyone else.

"Anyway…" he said, pulling a hand through his hair again and continuing, "you proved that you don't have any ties to Epidemic or his crew. You don't play by any rules but your own and I like that. I *trust* that," he emphasized. "All I need to know now is what the rules are."

"So, you attacked me and my crew just to kidnap me and ask?"

"No," he said, his jaw clenching. "That wasn't my call. That attack was all Zentrith."

"I thought you said *you* were the captain of this ship."

"*Interim* captain," he corrected, clenching his fists. "I was just the first mate until about ten cycles ago."

"Oh?"

"Yeah," he said, scoffing. "When you chopped off Howard Wright's head, Epidemic decided he wanted to get rid of you. And since our ship was already in the Argenster Galaxy and on course to cross paths with your ship, we were the unlucky ones who got commandeered for this plan. And when our captain refused to abdicate his role and order us to attack you, Zentrith killed him for it." Rex glanced away and sucked his teeth. "That walking abomination was only assigned to our ship because of *you*."

Rex balled his fists as they rested on his knees. He tried to keep his voice even, but I was misery's favorite company to keep — I would recognize it anywhere, even when it was with someone else. And the death of a beloved captain? Being forced into a role he hadn't been expecting?

Rex and I had a lot more in common than I'd originally thought.

But that wasn't enough to sway me into doing what he wanted.

"Are you tying to guilt trip me right now?"

"I'm just giving you the facts," Rex said, scoffing. "And the fact is, you killed Howard Wright and caught Epidemic's attention. He tends to deal with problems while they're still…" he let his eyes crawl over me before shrugging, "not a threat, and Zentrith is the one who makes sure his problems never grow to be one."

"Is that so?" I asked, nodding. "I see."

"Do you?"

"Clearly," I said. "You want my help because you know I don't work for the person you're trying to get away from. Which tells me," I said, leaning forward again, "that you don't trust anyone in your life. You were forced to take a gamble on a stranger like me, and you're sitting there, praying to whatever god you believe in, that I don't disappoint. That you made the right choice." I nodded again. "I see a lot, Rex. But you misunderstood one very important fact about me."

"And that would be?"

"I am absolutely the threat your little *supernova* thinks I am," I said, smiling at him. Rex's eyes grew wide, and it was almost comical to watch his face as his mind connected the dots of what I was implying.

"Then…"

"I plan to kill Zentrith and Epidemic and every other sentient organism that had a hand in killing my husband."

"Seriously?"

"Do I give you the impression that I'm making a joke?"

Silence.

I could only guess what was going through Rex's mind, but in truth, his thoughts didn't interest me. What did interest me was Zentrith — how he'd known what galaxy *The Reveler* would be flying through, when we'd be flying through it, and how he'd known in enough time to commandeer a ship close enough to intercept us. A dangerous thought bloomed in my mind, and I tried not to water it too much, but it had taken root long before Zentrith had dragged us back to this ship.

"That makes this easy, then," Rex said, cutting into my thoughts and drawing my attention back to him. "It seems like our goals align. So, do we have a deal?"

"Do we?" I asked, lifting my brows. "What goals do we have in common?"

"The safety of my sisters and your crew," he said, holding up a finger as he listed his reasons. "Getting all of you off this ship and back onto yours. Killing Zentrith."

I grinned at that last one.

"I'm inclined to agree with you, but there's a few things I need to know first."

"Like what?"

"Who are your sisters?"

"Does that matter?" Rex asked, lifting his brows.

"It absolutely does," I said, laughing. "If you think I'm accepting just anyone onto my ship, you're crazy."

I didn't give him any more information than that, but the power dynamic aboard *The Reveler* was already tenuous, at best. I'd been making progress with earning the respect of the crew as their captain, but I was a long way away from receiving the unwavering loyalty that Xavier had. And it would defeat the purpose of getting back to the ship only to have my authority undermined by some newcomers who were loyal to a different captain.

It might seem like a trivial question to Rex, but his answer would determine if this deal fell through or not.

"You've met them," he said. "Zoek and Olexia."

"What are their skills?" I asked. When he lifted his brows, I shrugged. "Look, everyone has a role on my ship. I can't just agree to bring back two freeloaders."

"Olexia is in training to be a huntress. She'll be valuable to you for sure, but Zoek is…" he sighed and rubbed at the back of his neck as he searched for words. "Zoek is just kind," he admitted. "She doesn't have any practical skills for sailing through space, but she's good at remembering things. She reads everything and knows a lot about a lot."

I nodded. I had no doubts that Olexia would fit in just fine. With Pia around, there'd be someone her own age to show her the ropes, and I had no doubts that between Sigurd and James they'd be able to keep her in line. She could help fill in the gaps in security our fight with *The Croceria* created. Zoek though… there was no clear place where she would fit in with the crew. But, from the way Rex talked, there was no clear place where she fit in here either.

"And what do I get if I agree to your terms?" I asked. "This is a deal, right?"

"If you agree to take my sisters with you when you return to your ship, I'll help you and your crewmate get back to your ship."

"After we kill Zentrith."

"We?" he repeated.

"He attacked me, killed members of my crew, and works for the man who killed my husband," I said, staring at him. "You didn't honestly think I was going to leave this ship while his head was still attached to his shoulders, did you?"

"I guess not," he said, chuckling and extending his hand. "So? Do we have a deal?"

"We do," I said, shaking his hand.

"Great," he sighed. "It's a pleasure to be working with you, Captain Johnson."

The name took me off guard.

Captain Johnson.

No one had ever called me that before, and the weight of the title dropped down on me like an anvil from a skyscraper. I crumbled beneath it, even as my back stiffened and I cleared my throat.

"I prefer Lady Kyra."

"Lady, huh?" Rex laughed as he pulled his hand back. "I guess that part is true, then."

"What's true?"

"It's nothing," he said, brushing aside the question as he pushed himself to his feet. "Allow me to correct myself. It's a pleasure to be working with you, Lady Kyra. I'm looking forward to seeing exactly what The Lady Widow can do."

11 HOURS

A CAPTIVE

The shift from prisoner to ally was unceremonious.

After we shook hands, Rex called Olexia and Pia back into the room to go over what would happen next. The plan was to divide and conquer: the girls would head toward the mech room while he and I headed for the control center on the main deck.

Unlike *The Reveler,* which had been getting consistent upgrades over the years thanks to Chise, Sigurd, and Pia, *The Croceria* was still at its base model. All the technology on the ship was housed in one room on the first level, and the first thing Zentrith had done when he arrived was install a signal jammer. It kept any communication that wasn't from Epidemic himself from getting in or out of the ship. It's why our translators hadn't worked to contact *The Reveler* despite Pia's upgrades to them.

I was a little hesitant about sending Pia into the depths of the croc's ship on her own, but she had a fire in her eyes that hadn't been there before. I don't know what she and Olexia discussed on the other side of

Rex's door, but it clearly sparked something to life in her. I didn't know what it was, but I wasn't about to snuff it out either. When Rex suggested the idea of sending her to the mech room with Olexia, she met my gaze and gave me the tiniest nod.

I agreed to let her go, but I sent Glupin with her just in case.

While they unjammed the ship, Rex and I would handle Zentrith. He was the source of both our woes, and while it was unlikely either of us could solo him in a fight, Rex had good reason to believe we could take him together.

"What we have on our side, Lady Kyra," he said, smirking over his shoulder as he led the way down the hall toward a concealed set of stairs, "is the element of surprise."

"Zentrith can't be that stupid."

The words were barely more than a whisper, but they rang through my head as if I'd shouted at the top of my lungs. After being surrounded by the constant scream of alarms, a quiet ship was both deafening and eerie. Rex had cut the alarms right before we parted ways with the girls. Pia and I couldn't see anything in the dark, but he and Olexia didn't have that problem, so they served as our guides through the dark.

I didn't like the idea of having to cling to Rex, but the alternative was to activate his orb. It was some gadget he'd found on a moon called Eenkit. Apparently, the planet itself was uninhabitable, so the residents lived on one of the dozen or so moons. It took the better part of five thousand cycles to orbit their planet and return to facing their sun, so they'd built countless other ways to source light. Rex's orb was just one of them. It fully charged in a few hours, lasted for days, and followed the nearest heat source around until it was put out. It was useful, but it wasn't discreet, and if we'd wanted to announce our presence, there were easier ways to go about it.

The only other option was to inch my way through the dark alone, and that would take hours. No one had time for that. So, I was left stumbling through the dark with Rex.

"Trust me, Zentrith is more brawn than brain," Rex muttered, gripping my elbow as he helped me up the stairs. "If I tell him the alarms were for that KUAF commander, he'll believe me. She's been plotting in that cell for weeks."

I'd forgotten about Shyanne.

If only for a few moments, it had been blissful.

Now, my chest tightened, and my hand dug into the muscles in Rex's arm. He didn't say anything, but I could feel the silence shifting to something awkward, and I loosened my grip on him.

"Why is she here?" I asked, trying to keep my voice even.

"She came with Zentrith," Rex said, shrugging beneath my hand. "But a decorated KUAF commander like her gets caught right when he shows up? My guess is that wasn't a mistake on her part."

"Decorated?" I repeated.

"You've never heard of her?"

"I'm from Star Prime 1307, remember?"

Rex chuckled. "She's pretty famous," he said. "She's known for breaking up alien trafficking rings in a dozen different galaxies. No one really wants to get on her bad side."

"If she's that recognizable, why would Zentrith bring her on board?"

"Like I said, more brawn than brain."

I simmered on Rex's words but said nothing else. If Shyanne was here, then I could only guess that she was hunting the same man I was, albeit for different reasons. Which meant she hadn't been lying when she told me I'd been *slithering through the wrong grass*. She wasn't here because of me, Pia, or Xavier — she was here for Zentrith and Epidemic, and that made me wrinkle my nose in the dark.

Somehow, knowing that Shyanne wasn't just some dumb airhead left a bad taste in my mouth.

It was bitter… like respect.

"What are you going to do with her when this is all over?"

"No idea."

"Why don't you send her with us?"

The question was out of my mouth before I even realized what I was suggesting. No part of me wanted Shyanne Olight, KUAF commander, and Xavier's baby mama, on my ship. Truly, I didn't want to be anywhere near her, but there were questions rotting in the pit of my stomach, and if I was ever going to have any hope of cutting them out, I needed answers — answers only she could give me.

"And why would I do that?"

"Because you've got your own mess to clean up, and she's one of mine."

"You know her?"

"By association," I said, working hard to keep my voice light. "We've got some unfinished business."

"Then she's all yours," he said. "Anything else you want to ask for while you've got me all alone at your mercy?"

The question was followed by a lighthearted chuckle as Rex glided his fingers over some kind of panel. It lit up with the same soft purple light we'd seen in the holding cell, and a door hissed open. We stepped into a narrow elevator that pulled us upward, leaving us staring at each other as we waited to arrive at our floor.

The lights from the panels cast a soft glow in the tiny space and lit up the left side of his face. It darkened all of his features, and his green eyes almost looked black as he stared at the lights showing our ascent to the top floor of the ship. I was enjoying the quiet, but there was one more question I wanted an answer to while he was being so forthcoming with information.

"Why did Zentrith go after Pia?"

"What?" Rex asked, dragging his gaze back to my face. "You mean the girl who came with you?" I nodded, and he laughed. "Yeah… she was just a side quest."

It was my turn to be confused.

"What?"

"Some rich merchant from Canaam paid for her eyes a while back. It was one of Howard's jobs, but I guess he never delivered?" Rex looked at me like I would have the answer, and all I could do was stare at him wide-eyed and in shock, but that didn't stop him from shrugging and continuing on. "I don't know who realized she was the same girl, but someone did, so Zentrith grabbed her. He was there for you, though."

"So you could chat me up?"

"So Epidemic could."

The words hung between us. They were heavy, but I couldn't bring myself to be anxious about them.

If Epidemic was paying that much attention to me, then I'd give him a show.

"Guess he won't be happy that you're letting me go."

"Not at all," Rex said, letting out a nervous laugh and rubbing the back of his neck. "But I'm not going to let my sisters get any deeper into this than they already are."

"You really care about them."

He barked out a laugh. "I guess so. But that's just what big brothers do, right?"

"I'm an only child, so I wouldn't know."

"You want me to be your big brother too, Lady Kyra?" he asked, smirking down at me. "I'll look out for you if you want."

I snorted and rolled my eyes. "I'd rather you kill the merchant who paid for Pia's eyes."

"And why would I do that?"

"Two sisters," I said, holding up my fingers. "Two favors."

The elevator slowed to a stop as Rex stared down at me. It made me aware for the first time of how close we were standing. I hadn't paid much attention to it, but the dark box suddenly felt too small for the both of us. There was barely any room to breathe without brushing up against each other, and he took another half step forward, removing what little space remained between us as he lowered his voice.

"Fine. If it's for you, Lady Kyra, I wouldn't mind killing a man or two."

"Great. Then it's settled," I said, pushing him back. "You don't need to be that close to me."

"Am I making you nervous?"

"You're pissing me off," I said, matching his lighthearted tone as he chuckled and led the way down the hall. It was a short walk from the elevator to the control room, and I let go of Rex as we neared it.

There was a single door leading inside with two narrow panes of clear panels on either side. They served as windows, and golden light spilled out of them as we passed by the sun of some solar system. The display panels filtered out the most harmful aspects of the light, but it was still more than enough to see the five people standing inside.

Zentrith was easy to recognize with his pitch-black scales and overwhelming height. He was like a behemoth standing in a toy spaceship. He stood next to a man I could only assume was the navigator since he was at the center of a raised platform with a control board shaped in a crescent arc. His fingers tapped and slid over either side of it like he was typing out a love letter to the stars.

He stood out compared to the others — looked more humanoid than croc. He was smaller than the rest of them, less intimidating. From what I could see, peeking through the panels, he was about my height, with a broad chest, round belly, and circular glasses. They slid down the edge of his nose, and he adjusted them before returning his focus to the control board. He had dark green scales that showed up in patches over his dark brown skin — on top of his hands, down the sides of his neck, at the corner of his green eyes, and across his cheeks like freckles.

I'd never seen anyone like him before, but he didn't seem like a fighter.

He was in a pale orange tactical suit that clashed with the dark blue ones Zentrith and the other crocs wore, and it only served to confirm my theory that different colors meant different things. It made me wonder what Zoek's silver one meant, and my eyes were drawn to her in the corner.

She sat with her hands crossed in her lap.

A humanoid creature with pale pink skin, one purple eye, and four arms leaned over her. Their fingers were fluid as they stitched up the side of Zoek's face with some kind of silvery thread. It shimmered in the light, and Zoek didn't flinch even once as the needle passed through her skin and pulled together the gashes left behind by Shyanne's teeth.

Shyanne sat on the floor next to them — her limbs bound, and a gag shoved into her mouth. Everything about her was disheveled, from her hair to her clothes to the angry red blotches and purple bruises spreading across her skin. She had one long gash carved into her left leg, but it was clear that she wasn't the priority. There was still fight and fire in her eyes as she lay on the ground, and the bitter taste of respect returned.

I hated it.

I pulled my attention away from Shyanne to meet Rex's gaze. Like me, he was pressed back against the wall and was using the window panels to assess the situation inside.

Part of me wanted to barge in there and start swinging Mandy around like the madwoman I felt like, but this was his ship — his crew. Of the five people in there, I knew two of them wouldn't be an issue. Zoek wasn't Rex's enemy, and Shyanne couldn't fight. There was no telling what the medic or navigator would do, though. It just depended on whose side they'd chosen to align themselves with — Rex or Zentrith.

He caught my eye and gave me a quick nod before closing his eyes and exhaling a slow breath.

Like Shyanne had earlier, his whole body began to shift. He'd been tall before, but his legs grew longer — thicker — scalier. The tactical suit he wore expanded with him, and I realized it served a function beyond my initial thoughts. Rex grew and expanded into a hulking croc with pitch-black scales, just like Zentrith, and I stared at him with wide eyes as he towered over me. His black suit on top of his black scales made Rex look like a demon shadow personified. His green eyes had morphed into a shimmering shade of gold, and that was the only thing that seemed to keep him from bleeding into the empty nothingness of space. He was more monster than man now, and if I hadn't seen him shift with my own two eyes, I wouldn't have believed I was looking at the same person.

He met my gaze, and I liked to imagine my face was blank, but I guess I didn't hide my shock all that well, because he winked down at me before pushing open the door to the control room and striding inside while I hung back outside.

Rex moved like a man who'd never kept much company with fear, because instead of offering up an explanation for the alarms — of pretending to still be on the same side — Rex walked up to Zentrith and uppercut him with all his strength.

And he was right — we did have the element of surprise on our side.

Zentrith was knocked off his feet, and that seemed to be the only invitation his crew needed to fly into motion.

Zoek grabbed Shyanne and the medic, and hauled them onto the platform with the navigator, away from the fight. The moment they landed there, he adjusted his glasses and pulled a black lever. A low hum vibrated the air, and a pale purple light rose from the ground and chased itself around the platform. As soon as it was up, Zoek grabbed Zentrith by his arm, twisted her body, kicked her leg out beneath his, and tossed him over her shoulder into the barrier.

He never saw it coming.

He let out a roar of frustration as he lit up like a Christmas tree. His body jerked and twisted and yanked in every direction until he finally fell off the barrier and landed on the ground. Rex tried to take the opportunity to kick him while he was down, but Zentrith was resilient.

He grabbed Rex's foot and yanked him forward, pulling him off balance. Zoek tried to push Zentrith back into the barrier, but he swung the back of his fist across her face, and she spun a full rotation before she crumpled to the ground. The navigator called her name, but he didn't move from the platform or drop the barrier. The medic fidgeted inside, pacing in a tight circle as they watched in silence — their one eye blinking rapidly as the scene unfolded.

Rex was their last hope, but it was becoming apparent why Rex had played along with Zentrith instead of fighting him from the start. They might've been the same size, but Zentrith wielded a kind of raw power that Rex just couldn't match. I could hear the blows landing against Rex's jaw.

Against his ribs.

Blood splattered across the console, and it was clear who the winner of this fight would be if nothing changed.

Rex put up a good fight — threw some good punches and caught

Zentrith with an elbow to the face and a knee to the gut, but it wasn't enough. Before long, Zentrith had Rex on the ground.

He straddled him and cackled as he drove his fist into Rex's face relentlessly. Rex put his guard up, but it was useless. Zentrith broke through it and landed blow after blow after blow.

My stomach churned just watching it, but this was the opportunity I'd been waiting for.

I slipped into the control room without a word. Every eye was glued to Rex and Zentrith, so no one noticed when I came in.

When I extended my stythe.

When I released the blade.

It was only after I'd stepped over to the platform, a finger pressed to my lips, that the navigator noticed me. His eyes locked with mine, and when I signaled for him to lower the barrier, he squinted at me.

There was no trust to be found in his gaze, and I didn't blame him. I was a stranger who could be on Zentrith's side for all he knew. And it wasn't like I had the time to explain anything. Not when Rex was literally being beaten to death before our eyes.

The stench of vomit and copper saturated the room. Crimson blood plastered the floor and dripped down the side of the barrier like some eccentric art decor, and the navigator couldn't stop Zentrith. Neither could the medic, and neither could Shyanne.

I was Rex's only hope, and we both knew that. So, with one more wild gesture to the barrier, he gave me a terse nod and lowered it.

I wasted no time climbing onto the platform and then onto the control board. Fragile buttons crunched beneath my boots, and a fiery rage rolled off the navigator in waves at my blatant disrespect, but I was grateful when he remained silent.

I needed the height — the leverage.

I angled the curve of my blade at Zentrith's head and sucked in a sharp breath before jumping and swinging it down as hard as I could.

Gravity did the rest of the work.

My stythe cut into the back of Zentrith's head and slid down his spine. He screamed like he was experiencing pain for the first time, and the biggest rush of pure dopamine hit my brain at the sound. It left me frozen as Zentrith reached around to swing behind him.

I wasn't fast enough to dodge it.

The back of his hand caught me in the chest, and I flew backward into the display panels. My head cracked against it, and I groaned as the taste of salty pennies filled my mouth. The control room spun, but it didn't matter.

Zentrith was on all fours as he struggled and failed to pry my stythe from his back. Adrenaline was a crazy thing if he could still move after that, but so could I. He had incredible strength, but his arms were too short to reach behind him, and something about that fact was so amusing to me.

Here was mister big, bad, and powerful, brought to his knees by my own hand.

I couldn't help but laugh at the sight as memories of being choked, manhandled, and mistreated by him flooded my mind. I staggered back to my feet and walked over to him, careful to avoid his flailing limbs. Rex was still rolling himself off the ground when I yanked my stythe free, readjusted my grip, and swung it again.

And again.

And again.

With each cut, Zentrith's screams got louder. They rose in tandem with my laughter, and I didn't stop until my joy was the only thing that remained.

Zentrith was slumped over on the floor, his back a mural of crimson blood, navy blue fibers, pink muscle, and white bone. Death turned him into art, and a sick sense of satisfaction burrowed itself into the marrow of my bones knowing that I'd created this twisted masterpiece.

I huffed as I stared down at him. Sweat dripped into my eye, and I blinked it away.

"Lady Kyra?"

The voice was soft and tentative and curious and familiar, but I ignored it. Instead, I stepped around his motionless body to look down at his face — to watch him wheezing as he clung to the last vestiges of life. His eyes were wide as he fought for breath, and I looked him in the eye as I smiled down at him.

"Enough of that," I whispered, lifting my blade. "Sleep."

12 HOURS

A CAPTIVE

Everything after I beheaded Zentrith was a blur.

Questions were fired at me one after another.

Who are you?

Where did you come from?

What just happened?

The medic, whose name I learned to be Qualwa, rushed over to Rex and Zoek. Rex was already sitting up on his own, hand to jaw and spitting out blood and teeth like it was a wad of old gum. He groaned, but he shooed Qualwa away, refusing to let them fuss over him until Zoek was awake and confirming that she was well.

Zoek sounded like nothing I expected. I'd heard her yell when she was fighting with Shyanne, but her normal voice was soft as clouds. Her words were light, airy, and gentle. It was a sharp contrast to the scar trailing across her face and her battle-worn attire. She looked like a scrappy street-fighter, but spoke like a queen. It was odd, but I respected a woman who could pull off that kind of duality.

The navigator never moved away from the control board or slowed down. I wouldn't be surprised if he were attached to the thing. Qualwa called him Drax, and for a brief moment, I entertained the idea of dragging him off the platform, just to see how he'd react. It was an amusing thought, but one I chose not to act on. No one had that kind of energy — not me, and especially not Rex. Every ounce of his laissez-faire demeanor was gone. All that was left were bloody lips, broken bones, and bruised egos. I asked if he was okay, but he only nodded and dragged himself over to a corner to lick his wounds.

Shyanne was still gagged, but her eyes never left me. I refused to look at her, but I could feel her hazel gaze following my every movement. I had no desire for that kind of scrutiny, but there was nothing to be done about it either — not like I could throw her back into a cell.

I had bigger things to worry about, like the sudden voices bickering in my head.

"Are you insane?"

Pia's voice carried a slight echo to it as it traveled through my translator. At some point, she and Olexia had been successful in unjamming the ship. She'd tried to explain what the situation had been — something about a syntho-something being welded to a carbo-thingy and blocking a communication transponder and yada-yada-yah.

The explanation wasn't for me.

"You know what, *no*," Sigurd said, the rage in his voice slowing his words. "You don't get to be mad at me when I tried to save your life."

"But you did nothing!"

"I followed an RZ-19 through three solar systems in a fighter pod!" Sigurd shouted back, forcing me to flinch at the volume. "Do you think that was fun for me, Piaseltra?"

Piaseltra? Was that her full name?

"You promised not to call me that anymore!" Pia screamed, groaning.

"Then don't give me a reason to," he shot back.

"Are you two done?" I asked, breaking into the argument. "Because as fun as this is, I'm actually exhausted and would like to figure out where our ship is, so..."

"Lady Kyra, are you okay?"

The question came from both of them, and it was kind of hilarious how they spoke at the same time — same inflections on my name — same worry lifting their question at the end. I wanted to laugh, but I worried the sound might give Rex and his crew PTSD. They were stealing glances at me like I'd lost the last traces of my mind as I stared out the display panel at the passing stars and talked to voices only I could hear.

Rex looked like he wanted to approach me, but Mandy was still in my hands. I'd put the blade away and leaned against the staff, but I'd taken Zentrith's head for myself and was tapping my foot against his forehead the same way I would a rock as I doled out my next orders.

"I'm fine," I promised Sigurd and Pia. "Just tired. Sigurd, where are you?"

"I'm tailing *The Croceria*."

"This whole time?"

"Yes," he said, sighing. "When the control center lost contact with your translator, they sent me to track you down. I followed you to the ship, but I ran into a few obstacles that kept me from boarding. I've been on your tail since."

"Impressive," I muttered, nodding to myself.

"At least someone appreciates my effort."

"You know what! I —"

"Don't start," I warned Pia. "Stay focused. Pia, can you get a signal to *The Reveler* from here?"

"I should be able to," she said. "I managed to connect our translators from here, so I don't see why I couldn't."

"Great. Bring your ship into the hangar bay, Sigurd. You can refuel, we can regroup, and we'll contact James from there. Pia, meet me down there."

"Understood."

Again, they spoke in unison, and I coughed out a laugh as it was finally, wonderfully, blissfully silent. No alarms. No fighting. No talking.

I could breathe for the first time, but there was still no time to relax. I stretched and collapsed Mandy back down to its original size and slapped it back onto my wrist. I had the attention of everyone in the room as soon as I did and smirked as I leaned down to pick up Zentrith's leaking head.

"You think I could get a bag for this?"

Ten minutes later, I was wedged into the fighter pod with Sigurd and Pia. There was only one seat inside, and Pia took it as she tinkered with the controls. Zentrith's head sat on what my exhausted mind could only equate to a dashboard. It had been dropped into a cloth bag and enclosed in an expanding jar. It was clear and round, and left Zentrith's head looking like a bloody snow globe.

Both Sigurd and Pia had cast wary glances at it when I arrived, but when I held it up and said, "It's Zentrith," they simply nodded and looked away. As if me beheading a man was a perfectly normal thing.

And maybe, at this point, it was?

Only time would tell.

"Hello?"

My head snapped up at the sound of James' voice. His words met us before the video feed did, and when he showed up as a tiny hologram standing in front of us, relief rushed through me. I almost wanted to cry, and I was grateful that he wasn't here, because had he been in front of me, I wouldn't have been able to stop myself from flinging myself into his arms for a hug.

And it hit me just how much I'd come to rely on James.

More than Xavier's first mate, he was mine too. These weren't the circumstances I wanted to realize how much I appreciated him, but I understood now more than ever that time is not promised to anyone. So, I made a mental note to put more effort into paying attention to him when we made it back to the ship — not just to train, but to talk. To genuinely understand the man my husband had called *brother*.

And not just him, the whole crew.

Pia's insubordination and the fight between Rex and Zentrith, had taught me something important: the crew's faith in their captain could mean the difference between life and death. We'd lucked out that Epidemic had wanted me and Pia alive — me to interrogate and her to sell her eyes to the highest bidder — but that wouldn't always be the case. And seeing the absolute faith Rex's crew had in him — how they'd moved without hesitation in that fight even though he'd only been their captain for ten cycles, gave them no warnings, no orders, and no explanations — showed me what a magnificent failure I was as a captain when the members of my ship wouldn't even vote to rescue me after I'd been captured.

It showed me how broken our crew was.

I didn't expect any easy fixes, but if I could start with the people closest to me already — getting to know James, Sigurd, Chise, and the triplets — then maybe we could start to fix some fundamental things.

Maybe we could all start to heal from Xavier's death.

It was a big hope, and it started with getting back to the ship. So, I called back out to James.

"Hey! Can you hear me?"

"Kyra!?"

"The one and only," I said, coughing out a laugh. "Did you miss me?"

"You have no idea," James said, returning my laugh with a strained yet relieved one of his own. "I'm glad you're okay."

"Making assumptions now?"

"You're alive and in one piece. You're fine," he said, rubbing a hand over his bald head. "You're fine."

I narrowed my eyes as he pulled a hand over his face and paced in a tight circle. James, for as long as I'd known him, had never been the type to get stressed out. He was the kind of man who was punctual and organized, and Xavier had frustrated him with his go-with-the-flow attitude on occasion, but he wasn't the pace back and forth and sigh deeply while scratching at his scalp kind of man.

Something was wrong.

"What's going on, James?" I asked, crossing my arms over the back of Pia's seat and leaning forward. "You're not acting like yourself."

"I don't feel like myself," he admitted, stopping in front of the screen. "Who's with you?"

"Sigurd and Pia?"

He nodded. "We need to speak privately."

I lifted my brows in surprise and glanced at the other two, who wore matching expressions of surprise. Sigurd recovered first and stepped toward the hatch.

"Come on, Pia."

"But —"

"Move it," he said, glaring at her. "This is between the captain and her first mate. Or do you somehow think you're entitled to every discussion she has now because you smoked with her a few times?"

Pia huffed and rolled her eyes and sucked her teeth and sighed and groaned and dragged her feet, but she still moved over to the hatch and shoved her way past Sigurd to go stand outside. He sighed and shook his head before turning his attention back to me.

"We'll be waiting outside," he said. "Shout if you need us."

I nodded and waited for the hatch to close behind them before shifting around to sit in the seat Pia had just vacated. I sank into it and every muscle in my body screamed with relief and exhaustion. I'd definitely pushed myself past my limits, but I still had a bit further to go.

"Hey," I said, gripping the armrests as I sat up in the seat and met James' holographic gaze. "It's just me now. What's up?"

"I'm sorry, Ky."

"What are you apologizing for?"

"Because…" he sighed and shook his head before steeling his nerves. "Because this wasn't an accident."

There it was.

He said what I'd been thinking the whole time.

"Someone leaked our intel to Epidemic," I said, nodding.

"You knew?"

"It wasn't hard to figure out once the pieces started coming together," I admitted, shrugging. "It's been an eventful couple of hours on this end."

"Same here."

"Then it seems like we have a lot to catch up on," I said, leaning back in the seat and blowing out a heavy breath of air.

"Can you give me the highlights?"

"Mmm…" I sighed, rubbing my forehead. "I killed Zentrith, allied with Captain Drexel C. Barnes, made a deal with him to bring his sisters on board, and put a hit out on some merchant on Canaam who wants to buy Pia's eyes," I said, trying to discern the relevant information from smaller details spiraling through my mind. "Oh," I added, sitting up so I could watch his facial expression shift, "I met Shyanne Olight. She's coming back with us."

"Oh."

His face was a perfect mask. He *definitely* knew about Shyanne.

"Yeah," I said, letting a dark chuckle shake its way out of me. "*Oh.*"

"Look, Ky…"

"I don't want to talk about it, Jay," I said, shaking my head. "Not right now. Just… give me the highlights. What's going on over there?"

"I think we should talk about that when you get back."

"Chickening out?"

"You've been through more than I expected."

"James, just tell me," I sighed, fighting back the growing irritation tugging at my bones. "I'm tired. I don't want any surprises."

He sighed again — heavier this time.

"After you and Pia were taken, and Sigurd went after you, I did some… investigating."

"And what did you find?"

"That your suspicion is right," he said, pulling a hand over his face. "I don't know when it started, or for how long, but someone on the crew is a traitor. I found encrypted messages to an information broker."

"Do you know who?" I asked.

"No. Our servers were wiped. I only found what I did because an error corrupted a file and left a trail. Pia might be able to dig in and find more, but…"

"Gotta rule out that the traitor isn't her or Sigurd," I said, giving voice to the doubt he didn't want to speak.

"Right."

"It's not them," I said, shaking my head. "I have no evidence to support that fact, but I know it's not them the same way I know it's not you. I've put my life in the hands of you three, and you've never given me reason to believe that was the wrong decision."

"I appreciate that."

I waved a hand at him as I leaned back in the seat.

A traitor.

Part of me wanted to be surprised that this had happened, but I couldn't muster up the energy to even pretend. Xavier's death hadn't been easy for anyone, and I hadn't helped. I'd failed as his wife and his successor, so I couldn't blame anyone for wanting to see me gone.

"What do you want to do?"

That was the million-dollar question, wasn't it? It seemed like James was asking me that all the time, but what did I want to do? Where did I want to go next? It was a lot of pressure, and most of the time I had no idea. I didn't know how this whole revenge thing was supposed to work, but I did know three things for certain.

One, this path of revenge and carnage wasn't one I was willing to turn away from.

Two, everyone wouldn't be willing to come on this journey with me.

And three, I was perfectly fine with that.

My path would form itself beneath my feet as I walked down it. Of that, I had no doubt. Now, I just needed to make sure there were no stumbling blocks in my way.

"How long did this detour set us back?" I asked.

"Maybe a cycle or two? Assuming you get back soon."

"Then we stay the course," I said. "We should have at least sixty cycles before we reach Shereve, right?"

"Give or take a few cycles, yes."

"Then we'll use that time to do some spring cleaning," I said, leaning forward and holding his gaze. "We'll figure out who the mole is. We'll cut its nose off since it wants to spite its face, and then we'll kick them and every other ill-content miscreant off at the next planet. But I'm the captain now, James," I whispered, glaring at the screen as unwieldy emotions bloomed in my chest and tried to choke my words. "The Lady of this ship. And I will *not* be a prisoner who lives in constant fear of being captured among the stars. So, if anyone wants to doubt me, fine. But they won't succeed in destroying all that Xavier built. And if they try," I grinned, and let out the laughter I'd been holding back, "I'll show them exactly why he left everything to me."

"Well said, Lady Kyra," James said, grinning. "I will await your safe return here. And when you arrive, we'll… how do you say it? Flip a few tables?"

I barked out a laugh at that.

"Sounds fun, James. I can't wait."

TO BE CONTINUED…

NEXT TIME ON

THE LADY WIDOW

MUTINY
AMONG THE STARS

COMING 2027

C. M. Lockhart (also known as Chelsea) writes books about Black girls who aren't all that nice. Her debut novel, *We Are the Origin*, was released June 2022, and her latest series, *The Lady Widow*, is her venture into the sci-fi genre. She is the owner of Written in Melanin, which encompasses a podcast and YouTube channel of the same name, founder of the Melanin Library, host of the Melanin Chat, contributing editor of *Magic in the Melanin: A Black Fantasy Anthology*, and co-founder of the DNF Book Club. More information can be found on her website, https://WrittenInMelanin.com

Thank you for reading *The Lady Widow: Captured Among the Stars*. If you enjoyed this book, please consider telling a friend about it and leaving a rating or review for it on Amazon, Goodreads, Storygraph, or your favorite bookish app of choice.

You can find more books by C. M. Lockhart on her website, CMLockhart.com

Thank you again and, until next time, may your days be lovely and your books full of melanin.

www.ingramcontent.com/pod-product-compliance
Lightning Source LLC
Chambersburg PA
CBHW061732050726
47598CB00002B/456